THE MAGAZINE OF
BIZARRO F

MW01168982

Issue #4

Guest Editor: John Skipp
Editor-in-Chief: Jeff Burk
Cover art by Carlton Mellick III
cover art copyright © 2010 Carlton Mellick III
Interior illustrations by Nick Gucker (pages 34—41)
interior illustration copyright @ 2010 Nick Gucker
Interior illustrations by Josh Meyer (pages 85—94)
interior illustration copyright © 2010 Josh Meyer
The Magazine of Bizarro Fiction
205 NE Bryant
Portland, OR 97211

Please send questions and comments to:
BizarroMagazine@gmail.com

www.BizarroCentral.com

Table of Contents

All Fiction Special Issue

PRETEND IT'S CANDY!
A Romantic Reach-Around
by Guest Editor John Skipp

Dear Awesome Freak of Nature That You Are—

I've been thinking a lot about you lately. Your restless mind. Your abnormal tastes. Your rage. Your joy. Your sense of dislocation. Your even greater sense of humor, in the face of it all.

Above all, your impatience with the world, as commonly (mis)represented. Your honest and justified hunger for something more . . . or at least a whole lot weirder.

Believe me: *I'm right there with ya*. Soooo weary of the tyranny of the tepid and tame. Done with the dumbass, unless it's really GREAT dumbass. Always itchy for the wise, startling gleam in the eye that tells me someone's up to something singular and wild.

That's where the weird hits the road.

And turns this into an adventure.

If you're the kind of freak I'm speaking of, then HAVE I GOT A TREAT FOR YOU! It's a scrumptious Bizarro Whitman's Sampler of willful mindfuckery and playful provocation, laid out like psychedelic chocolates on an endlessly shape-shifting meatplastic tray, replete with veins that pulse and jiggle.

Subversive snacks, to be devoured at your leisure.

Little brain-blasting bon bons of strange delight.

You can gobble 'em all at once, or savor them one at a time. (I recommend the order I put 'em in, but that's only a serving suggestion.) You can read 'em on the bus, on your lunch break, on the toilet, just before you go to sleep or right after you wake up.

That's the glory of the self-contained short story (which I'm thinking should by all rights be *the literature of choice*, in this speeded-up, no-time-for-anything world). You can swallow it whole in fifteen minutes: sometimes a little more, oft-times a whole lot less.

If Bizarro novels and novellas are the literary equivalent of the "cult" section in a really cool video store, then these stories are the literary equivalent of Adult Swim cartoons, or an early R. Crumb comic, or a painting by some mad surrealist fucker like Mark Ryden, Robert Williams or Salvador Dali. They walk in and go BOOM! with miniature genius writ large. Or full-blown genius in miniature, which is more to the point.

That's why it's such a thrill for me to guest edit the fiction end of this issue, and bring you this ginormous gift, which will keep on giving for years to come.

If there's one thing I love, it's when an authentic weirdo finds their genuine voice. And having found it, figures out a way to get that weird voice heard.

Bizarro fiction is forging a new home for these kinds of voices and visions. Setting up venues. Creating a scene. Whipping up excitement, inspiration, and hope. Not to mention a vivacious, "Merry Prankster"-like community of full-tilt devout art mutants I'm almost inordinately proud to have been welcomed inside of.

Turns out I was part of this scene the whole time: a connective tissue, or pulsating vein, subcutaneously linking what came before with what's coming up next, in my own little ways.

So it is with great love and honor and joy that I bring you these crazy-ass stories. Introducing some new writers that knocked me out, and providing a fresh showcase for some fellow freaks you may already know well.

All confecting a little something special, to incite and beguile you in unforeseen ways.

If that ain't foreplay, I don't know what is.

I also brought flowers. But they all have teeth.

Big love and nimble fingers,

—Skipp

Fuck it. Let's open with clowns: the default setting on mockable humanity, turned somehow waaaaay more distressing than they were ever meant to be. Probably because they're a mirror that shames us: the scariest joke of all.

Robert wrote this story at Clarion West back in 1990, and I heard him read it aloud shortly after. His screwball combination of scholarly gnosis, mad language skills, and batshit insanity made me an instant fan for life.

Bizarro well before the term was applied, this berserk noir riff on I Pagliacci brings that soap-impaired opera back to its greasy white-faced roots. "Once the bicycle-honker and rubber-chicken sex came to me," he says, "the rest of it fell into place."

Ridi Bobo
by Robert Devereaux

At first little things niggled at Bobo's mind: the forced quality of Kiki's mimed chuckle when he went into his daily pratfall getting out of bed; the great care she began to take painting in the teardrop below her left eye; the way she idly fingered a pink puffball halfway down her shiny green suit. Then more blatant signals: the creases in her crimson frown, a sign, he knew, of real discontent; the bored arcs her floppy shoes described when she walked the ruff-necked piglets; a wistful shake of the head when he brought out their favorite set of shiny steel rings and invited her, with the artful pleas of his expressive white gloves, to juggle with him.

But Bobo knew it was time to seek professional help when he whipped out his rubber chicken and held it aloft in a stranglehold—its eyes X'd shut in fake death, its pitiful head lolled against the back of his glove—and all Kiki could offer was a soundless yawn, a fatigued cock of her conical nightcap, and the curve of her back, one lazy hand waving bye-bye before collapsing languidly beside her head on the pillow. No honker would be brought forth that evening from her deep hip pocket,

though he could discern its outline there beneath the cloth, a coy maddening shape that almost made him hop from toe to toe on his own. But he stopped himself, stared forlornly at the flaccid fowl in his hand, and shoved it back inside his trousers.

He went to check on the twins, their little gloved hands hugging the blankets to their chins, their perfect snowflake-white faces vacant with sleep. People said they looked more like Kiki than him, with their lime-green hair and the markings around their eyes. Beautiful boys, Jojo and Juju. He kissed their warm round red noses and softly closed the door.

In the morning, Bobo, wearing a tangerine apron over his bright blue suit, watched Kiki drive off in their new rattletrap Weezo, thick puffs of exhaust exploding out its tailpipe. Back in the kitchen, he reached for the Buy-Me Pages. Nervously rubbing his pate with his left palm, he slalomed his right index finger down the Snooper listings. Lots of flashy razz-ma-tazz ads, lots of zingers to catch a poor clown's attention. He needed simple. He needed quick. Ah! His finger thocked the entry short and solid as a raindrop on a roof; he noted the address and slammed the book shut.

Bobo hesitated, his fingers on his apron bow. For a moment the energy drained from him and he saw his beloved Kiki as she'd been when he married her, honker out bold as brass, doing toe hops in tandem with him, the shuff-shuff-shuff of her shiny green pants legs, the ecstatic ripples that passed through his rubber chicken as he moved it in and out of her honker and she bulbed honks around it. He longed to mimic sobbing, but the inspiration drained from him. His shoulders rose and fell once only; his sweep of orange hair canted to one side like a smart hat.

Then he whipped the apron off in a tangerine flurry, checked that the boys were okay playing with the piglets in the backyard, and was out the front door, floppy shoes flapping toward downtown.

Momo the Dick had droopy eyes, baggy pants, a shuffle to his walk, and an office filled to brimming with towers of blank paper, precariously tilted—like gaunt placarded and stilted clowns come to dine—over his splintered desk. Momo wore a battered old derby and mock-sighed a lot, like a bloodhound waiting to die.

He'd been decades in the business and had the dust to prove it. As soon as Bobo walked in, the tramp-wise clown seated behind the desk glanced once at him, peeled off his derby, twirled it, and very slowly very deliberately moved a stiffened fist in and out of it. Then his hand opened—red nails, white fingers thrust out of burst gloves—as if to say, Am I right?

Bobo just hung his head. His clownish hands drooped like weights at the ends of his arms.

The detective set his hat back on, made sympathetic weepy movements—one hand fisted to his eye—and motioned Bobo over. An unoiled drawer squealed open, and out of it came a puff of moths and a bulging old scrapbook. As Momo turned its pages, Bobo saw lots of illicit toe hops, lots of swollen honkers, lots of rubber chickens poking where they had no business poking. There were a whole series of pictures for each case, starting with a photo of his mopey client, progressing to the flagrante delicto evidence, and ending, almost without exception, in one of two shots: a judge with a shock of pink hair and a huge gavel thrusting a paper reading DIVORCE toward the adulterated couple, the third party handcuffed to a Kop with a tall blue hat and a big silver star on his chest; or two corpses, their floppy shoes pointing up like warped surfboards, the triumphant spouse grinning like weak tea and holding up a big pistol with a BANG! flag out its barrel, and Momo, a hand on the spouse's shoulder, looking sad as always and not a little shocked at having closed another case with such finality.

When Bobo broke down and mock-wept, Momo pulled out one end of a checkered hanky and offered it. Bobo cried long and hard, pretending to dampen yard upon yard of the unending cloth. When he was done, Momo reached into his desk drawer, took out a sheet with the word CONTRACT at the top and two X'd lines for signatures, and dipped a goose-quill pen into a large bottle of ink. Bobo made no move to take it but the old detective just kept holding it out, the picture of patience, and drops of black ink fell to the desktop between them.

Momo tracked his client's wife to a seedy Three-Ring Motel off the beaten path. She hadn't been easy to tail. A sudden rain had come up and the pennies that pinged off his windshield had reduced visibility by half, which made the eager Weezo hard to keep up with. But Momo managed it. Finally, with a sharp right and a screech of tires, she turned into the motel parking lot. Momo slowed to a stop, eying her from behind the brim of his sly bowler. She parked, climbed up out of the tiny car like a soufflé rising, and rapped on the door of Room Five, halfway down from the office.

She jiggled as she waited. It didn't surprise Momo, who'd seen lots of wives jiggle in his time. This one had a pleasingly sexy jiggle to her, as if she were shaking a cocktail with her whole body. He imagined the bulb of her honker slowly expanding, its bell beginning to flare open in anticipation of her little tryst. Momo felt his bird stir in his pants, but a soothing pat or two to his pocket and a few deep sighs put it back to sleep. There was work afoot. No time nor need for the wild flights of his long-departed youth.

After a quick reconnoiter, Momo went back to the van for his equipment. The wooden tripod lay heavy across his shoulder and the black boxy camera swayed like the head of a willing widow as he walked. The rest—unexposed plates, flash powder, squeezebulb—Momo carried in a carpetbag in his free hand. His down-drawn mouth puffed silently from the exertion, and he cursed the manufacturers for refusing to scale down their product, it made it so hard on him in the inevitable chase.

They had the blinds down but the lights up full. It made sense. Illicit lovers liked to watch themselves act naughty, in Momo's experience, their misdoings fascinated them so. He was in luck. One wayward blind, about chest high, strayed leftward, leaving a rectangle big enough for his lens. Miming stealth, he set up the tripod, put in a plate, and sprinkled huge amounts of glittery black powder along his flashbar. He didn't need the flashbar, he knew that, and it caused all manner of problem for him, but he had his pride in the aesthetics of picture-taking, and he was willing to blow his cover for the sake of that pride. When the flash went off, you knew you'd taken a picture; a quick bulb squeeze in

the dark was a cheat and not at all in keeping with his code of ethics.

So the flash flared, and the smoke billowed through the loud report it made, and the peppery sting whipped up into Momo's nostrils on the inhale. Then came the hurried slap of shoes on carpet and a big slatted eyelid opened in the blinds, out of which glared a raging clownface. Momo had time to register that this was one hefty punchinello, with muscle-bound eyes and lime-green hair that hung like a writhe of caterpillars about his face. And he saw the woman, Bobo's wife, honker out, looking like the naughty fornicator she was but with an overlay of uh-oh beginning to sheen her eyes.

The old adrenaline kicked in. The usually poky Momo hugged up his tripod and made a mad dash for the van, his carpetbag shoved under one arm, his free hand pushing the derby down on his head. It was touch and go for a while, but Momo had the escape down to a science, and the beefy clown he now clouded over with a blanket of exhaust—big lumbering palooka caught off-guard in the act of chicken stuffing—proved no match for the wily Momo.

Bobo took the envelope and motioned

Momo to come in, but Momo declined with a hopeless shake of the head. He tipped his bowler and went his way, sorrow slumped like a mantle about his shoulders. With calm deliberation Bobo closed the door, thinking of Jojo and Juju fast asleep in their beds. Precious boys, flesh of his flesh, energetic pranksters, they deserved better than this.

He unzippered the envelope and pulled out the photo. Some clown suited in scarlet was engaged in hugger-mugger toe hops with Kiki. His rubber chicken, unsanctified by papa church, was stiff-necked as a rubber chicken can get and stuffed deep inside the bell of Kiki's honker. Bobo leaned back against the door, his shoes levering off the rug like slapsticks. He'd never seen Kiki's pink rubber bulb swell up so grandly. He'd never seen her hand close so tightly around it nor squeeze with such ardency. He'd never *ever* seen the happiness that danced so brightly in her eyes, turning her painted tear to a tear of joy.

He let the photo flutter to the floor. Blessedly it fell facedown. With his right hand he reached deep into his pocket and pulled out his rubber chicken, sad purple-yellow bird, a male's burden in this world. The sight of it brought back memories of their wedding. They'd had it performed by Father Beppo in the center ring of the Church of Saint Canio. It had been a beautiful day, balloons so thick the air felt close under the bigtop. Father Beppo had laid one hand on Bobo's rubber chicken, one on Kiki's honker, inserting hen into honker for the first time as he lifted his long-lashed eyes to the heavens, wrinkle lines appearing on his meringue-white forehead. He'd looked to Kiki, then to Bobo, for their solemn nods toward fidelity.

And now she'd broken that vow, thrown it to the wind, made a mockery of their marriage.

Bobo slid to the floor, put his hands to his face, and wept. Real wet tears this time, and that astonished him, though not enough—no, not nearly enough—to divert his thoughts from Kiki's treachery. His gloves grew soggy with weeping. When the flood subsided, he reached down and turned the photo over once more, scrutinizing the face of his wife's lover. And then the details came together—the ears, the mouth, the chin; oh God no, the hair and the eyes—and he knew Kiki and this bulbous-nosed bastard had been carrying on for a long time, a very long time indeed. Once more he inventoried the photo, frantic with the hope that his fears were playing magic tricks with the truth.

But the bald conclusion held.

At last, mulling things over, growing outwardly calm and composed, Bobo tumbled his eyes down the length of the flamingo-pink carpet, across the spun cotton-candy pattern of the kitchen floor, and up the cabinets to the Jojo-and-Juju-proofed top drawer.

Bobo sat at his wife's vanity, his face close to the mirror. Perfume atomizers jutted up like minarets, thin rubber tubing hanging down from them and ending in pretty pink squeezebulbs Bobo did his best to ignore.

He'd strangled the piglets first, squealing the life out of them, his large hands thrust beneath their ruffs. Patty Petunia had pistoned her trotters against his chest more vigorously and for a longer time than had Pepper, to Bobo's surprise, she'd always seemed so much the frailer of the two. When they lay still, he took up his carving knife and sliced open their bellies, fixed on retrieving the archaic instruments of comedy. Just as his tears had shocked him, so too did the deftness of his hands—guided by instinct he'd long supposed atrophied—as they removed the bladders, cleansed them in the water trough, tied them off, inflated them, secured each one to a long thin bendy dowel. He'd left Kiki's dead pets sprawled in the muck of their pen, flies growing ever more interested in them.

Sixty-watt lights puffed out around the perimeter of the mirror like yellow honker bulbs. Bobo opened Kiki's cosmetics box and took out three squat shallow cylinders of color. The paint seemed like miniature seas, choppy and wet, when he unscrewed and removed the lids.

He'd taken a tin of black paint into the boys' room—that and the carving knife. He sat beside Jojo in a sharp jag of moonlight, listening to the card-in-bike-spoke duet of their snores, watching their fat wide lips flutter like stuck bees. Bobo dolloped one white finger with darkness, leaning in to X a cross over Jojo's right eyelid. If only they'd stayed asleep. But they woke. And Bobo could not help seeing them in new light. They sat up in mock-stun, living outcroppings of Kiki's cruelty, and Bobo could not stop himself from finger-scooping thick gobs of paint and smearing their faces entirely in black. But even that was not enough for his distracted mind, which spiraled upward into bloody revenge, even though it meant carving his way through innocence. By the time he plunged the blade into the sapphire silk of his first victim's suit, jagging open downward a bloody furrow, he no longer knew which child he murdered. The other one led him a merry chase through the house, but Bobo scruffed him under the cellar stairs, his shoes windmilling helplessly as Bobo hoisted him up and sank the knife into him just below the second puffball. He'd tucked them snug beneath their covers, Kiki's brood; then he'd tied their rubber chickens together at the neck and nailed them smackdab in the center of the heartshaped headboard.

Bobo dipped a brush into the cobalt blue, outlined a tear under his left eye, filled it in. It wasn't perfect but it would do.

As horsehair taught paint how to cry, he surveyed in his mind's eye the lay of the living room. Everything was in readiness: the bucket of crimson confetti poised above the front door; the exploding cigar he would light and jam into the gape of her mouth; the tangerine apron he'd throw in her face, the same apron that hung loose now about his neck, its strings snipped off and spilling out of its big frilly kangaroo pouch; the Deluxe Husband-Tamer Slapstick he'd paddle her bottom with, as they did the traditional high-stepping divorce chase around the house; and the twin bladders to buffet her about the ears with, just to show her how serious things were with him. But he knew, nearly for a certainty, that none of these would stanch his blood lust, that

it would grow with each antic act, not assuaged by any of them, not peaking until he plunged his hand into the elephant's-foot umbrella stand in the hallway and drew forth the carving knife hidden among the parasols—whose handles shot up like cocktail toothpicks out of a ripple of pink chiffon—drew it out and used it to plumb Kiki's unfathomable depths.

Another tear, a twin of the first, he painted under his right eye. He paused to survey his right cheekbone, planning where precisely to paint the third.

Bobo heard, at the front door, the rattle of Kiki's key in the lock.

Momo watched aghast.

He'd brushed off with a dove-white handkerchief his collapsible stool in the bushes, slumped hopelessly into it, given a mock-sigh, and found the bent slat he needed for a splendid view of the front hallway and much of the living room, given the odd neck swivel. On the off-chance that their spat might end in reconciliation, Momo'd also positioned a tall rickety stepladder beside Bobo's bedroom window. It was perilous to climb and a balancing act and a half not to fall off of, but a more leisurely glimpse of Kiki's lovely honker in action was, he decided, well worth the risk.

What he could see of the confrontation pleased him. These were clowns in their prime, and every swoop, every duck, every tumble, tuck, and turn, was carried out with consummate skill. For all the heartache Momo had to deal with, he liked his work. His clients quite often afforded him a front row seat at the grandest entertainments ever staged: spills, chills, and thrills, high passion and low comedy, inflated bozos pin-punctured and deflated ones puffed up with triumph. Momo took deep delight—though his forlorn face cracked nary a smile—in the confetti, the exploding cigar, what he could see and hear of their slapstick chase. Even the bladder-buffeting Bobo visited upon his wife strained upward at the down-droop of Momo's mouth, he took such fond joy in the old ways, wishing with deep soundless sighs that more clowns these days would re-embrace them.

His first thought when the carving knife flashed in Bobo's hand was that it was rubber, or retractable. But there was no drawn-out scene played, no mock-death here; the blow came swift, the blood could not be mistaken for ketchup or karo syrup, and Momo learned more about clown anatomy than he cared to know—the gizmos, the coils, the springs that kept them ticking; the organs, more piglike than clownlike, that bled and squirted; the obscure voids glimmering within, filled with giggle power and something deeper. And above it all, Bobo's plunging arm and Kiki's crimped eyes and open arch of a mouth, wide with pain and drawn down at the corners by the weight of her dying.

Momo drew back from the window, shaking his head. He vanned the stool, he vanned the ladder. There would be no honker action tonight. None, anyway, he cared to witness. He reached deep into the darkness of the van, losing his balance and bellyflopping so that his legs flew up in the night air and his white shanks were exposed from ankle to knee. Righting himself, he sniffed at the red carnation in his lapel, took the inevitable faceful of water, and shouldered the pushbroom he'd retrieved.

The neighborhood was quiet. Rooftops, curved in high hyperbolas, were silvered in moonlight. So too the paved road and the cobbled walkways that led up to the homes on Bobo's side of the street. As Momo made his way without hurry to the front door, his shadow eased back and forth, covering and uncovering the brightly lit house as if it were the dark wing of the Death Clown flapping casually, silently, overhead. He hoped Bobo would not yank open the door, knife still dripping, and fix him in the red swirl of his crazed eyes. Yet maybe that would be for the best. It occurred to Momo that a world which contained horrors like these might happily be left behind. Indeed, from one rare glimpse at rogue-clown behavior in his youth, as well as from gruesome tales mimed by other dicks, Momo thought it likely that Bobo, by now, had had the same idea and had brought his knife-blade home.

This case had turned dark indeed. He'd have lots of shrugging and moping, much groveling and kowtowing to do, before this was over. But that came, Momo knew, with the territory. Leaning his tired bones into the pushbroom, he swept a swatch of moonlight off the front stoop onto the grass. It was his duty, as a citizen and especially as a practitioner of the law, to call in the Kops. A few more sweeps and the stoop was moonless; the lawn to either side shone with shattered shards of light. He would finish the walkway, then broom away a spill of light from the road in front of Bobo's house, before firing the obligatory flare into the sky.

Time enough then to endure the noises that would tear open the night, the clamorous bell of the mismatch-wheeled pony-drawn firetruck, the screaming whistles in the bright red mouths of the Kops clinging to the Kop Kar as it raced into the neighborhood, hands to their domed blue hats, the bass drums booming as Bobo's friends and neighbors marched out of their houses, spouses and kids, poodles and ponies and piglets highstepping in perfect columns behind.

For now, it was enough to sweep moonlight from Bobo's cobbled walkway, to darken the wayward clown's doorway, to take in the scent of a fall evening and gaze up wistfully at the aching gaping moon.

Oh, the children. WHAT ABOUT THE CHILDREN? It's a tough time to have one, a tough time to be one, a tough time to even think about the fact that they keep happening.

Here to put it all in the most deranged perspective available is trans-dimensional Bill Cosby-and-meat enthusiast Cameron Pierce.

"As far as the story goes," he says, "I scribbled it out in a mad fury one morning after 'Mickey Mouse is Dead' by the Subhumans got stuck in my head. I was eighteen, and full of words." And that says it all for me.

I am Meat, I am in Daycare
by Cameron Pierce

When Ted Branson called to ask the rate for Susan's daycare service, she never realized his child was a slab of meat. Now the man pushed her aside and lugged his meat-child into her house. "Name's Mr. Branson, but call me Ted," he said. "Should I put him with the other kids, or will you take him from here?"

"Mr. Branson . . . Ted," Susan said, "I can't take your child. I'm sorry, it's just not . . ."

She did not want to take the meat, but she could not offend this man. He might have friends with kids, although she doubted he had friends. Who would hang out with a guy who called meat his child? Well, if she was paid to watch kids and this lunatic wanted to pay her to babysit a hunk of cow, she would do it.

"I don't see what the problem could be."

Susan smiled. "Problem? There's no problem here. Bring your son this way and I'll introduce him to the other children."

"Scotty," Ted said.

"Excuse me?"

"My boy's name is Scotty."

"Oh, of course," said Susan. "His name is Scotty."

For the first time, Susan was glad the seven children she watched were, without exception, idiots.

She led Mr. Branson into the living room. The man dragged the hunk of meat behind him as if it were a reluctant child. Where the hell had the meat come from anyway? Maybe it was just a large rib-eye steak, but Susan had never seen rib-eyes that size before. She watched the seven children watching Alice in Wonderland, their comatose eyes reflecting the purple visage of the Cheshire Cat. "Everyone," she said. "Everyone, I'd like you to meet Scotty."

Haley, a little blonde girl, turned from the television and waved her hands like someone trying to signal a lifeguard. The other kids heard nothing, or pretended to hear nothing.

Children were such little creeps.

Normally, there were over ten pages of paperwork to fill out for a new child, but since Scotty wasn't really a child, she skipped the paperwork.

"Well," Mr. Branson said, "I'm late for work. If there are any forms to sign, I'll fill them out this evening, around five. Thanks again."

He kissed Susan on the cheek. He walked out of the living room. The front door slammed. Susan realized she had forgotten to ask how Mr. Branson found her daycare.

She heard the door creak and open up again. Mr. Branson called, "I forgot to tell you, Scotty's allergic to chocolate milk."

The door shut. Susan rubbed her left cheek, the one he had not kissed. She stared at the meat-child. She felt the kick of queasy memories in her gut, things she could not think about for the life of her.

Allergic to chocolate milk . . .

She expected to have an easier time lugging Scotty the meat-child into the kitchen. He could not have weighed more than sixty pounds, but felt at least double that. When she lifted him up, legs—which she hadn't seen—uncurled from the thing's red belly. She recoiled, dropping him. She fled to the kitchen and pressed up against the refrigerator. *Take care of the child, take care of the child, take care of the child*, she told herself. *Breathe in, breathe out.*

She returned with oven mitts. She stood over the meat-child, clamping and unclamping the mitts like a cottony lobster.

None of the other children said anything as Susan dragged Scotty into the kitchen by his legs. Susan wondered what the little idiots would tell their parents about Scotty, the new boy. She figured most would not remember anything at all. They would recall nothing about meat.

Scotty was too heavy for Susan to lift onto the kitchen table. Instead, she slid him into the corner, beside Tanuki's food and water. She emptied the water bowl, gone green with sedation, into the sink. She cursed her husband for the empty bottle of Jack he'd left out on the counter. The prick was a drinker these days, ever since the cat died. She understood how much he loved Tanuki. She loved Tanuki too. They had adopted the cat thirteen years ago, before they were even married. Now the cat

had been dead for over a year. Leaving food and water out was a means of coping that didn't hurt anyone, but if a parent were to see the empty whiskey bottle and complain to the daycare board, Susan could lose her business.

She tried her best to scrape the grime from the bowl but gave up after a half-assed attempt. She set the bowl on the counter. She searched the fridge for chocolate syrup. She realized it was no use. They were out of milk. She grabbed one of her Atkins chocolate-flavored protein shakes.

It was close enough, right?

Susan popped the tab and poured the thick, brown liquid into the bowl. She set the bowl on the floor next to Scotty. "Drink up," she said, but who was she kidding? She was talking to some fucking meat.

She lifted the bowl and tilted it just enough. A few drops splattered on the meat child's back. Nothing happened, so she poured more. Then she let the whole thing spill.

Still, nothing happened.

Susan left the chocolate-soaked Scotty on the linoleum floor and walked out of the kitchen. She peeked into the living room to make sure the kids were alright. Silent as crabs, the children stared at the television screen. The children seemed no less alive than before, but they had gone red and it wasn't from the movie's glow.

Susan screamed at these *new* children. She collapsed on the floor and choreographed an Ian Curtis nightmare. A very bad . . .

"Mrs. Mackery," said Charlie, the oldest boy she watched.

Susan looked up. Her insides tightened. A trail of crimson ran from the sofa where Charlie had sat to where he stood. The child gave no indication that he realized he was skinless. *How could he be without skin? How could he be alive?*

"Mrs. Mackery," he said.

"What is it, Charlie?" she said. When facing terrible situations, Susan knew to act normal. Acting normal was the key to overcoming all of life's problems.

"That new boy, he hurt me."

Susan looked at the other children. She looked at the cable box. 1:11 glowed green. How could it be over an hour past noon? Mr. Branson dropped off Scotty around eight. In that time, she had done nothing except drag the meat into the kitchen and pour the chocolate shake over it. Something wasn't right. Susan thought she might call her husband. He took care of every problem.

Something moved in the hallway. She looked at the children again, taking count. One was missing. Who? She registered their faces.

Haley.

"Haley," she called, "Haley!"

The toilet flushed. The sink ran for a few seconds, then the bathroom door opened. "Haley," she said.

The thing that scuttled into the living room was not Haley, even if it wore her face. It grinned, but the skull beneath failed to smile in sync with the loosely draped little girl face. Susan imagined more than one mind existing behind that hideous face.

In the kitchen there was a terrible crying, like a cat meowing, hung by its tail from a basketball hoop, swinging like a furry piñata, then beaten with metal bats into a sad and voiceless thing. *Everything and everyone was crying.*

Susan awoke in her bed. The light
overhead made her jaw ache. Her husband stood over her. He squinted at her. She felt pitiful and ashamed. He held out his hand and she took it.

"Where are the children?" she said.

He pulled her to her feet. "A new business offer came in so I took the day off. You were passed out like a sorority bitch. I called the parents. The children are gone. They'll be back. Are you hungry? I cooked dinner."

Of course they'll be back, Susan thought. Her guts mumbled. She had eaten nothing all day. "Did you have a bad day?" she said. *Would he ask about her day?*

He kissed her cheek, moving away from her as he did so. He turned off the light on his way out.

No, of course not.

Susan forced herself out of bed. She wanted to explain everything.

When she entered the kitchen, she felt scrambled in a fog. Mr. Branson stood from his seat at the table. "What the hell is he doing here?" she said.

Her husband turned around. "Ted is my partner. We're going into a sort of…new business together."

"What kind of business?" she demanded.

Her husband and Mr. Branson responded together. "Your new husband," they said.

The doorbell rang and Susan knew she must answer it, if only to escape from her husband and Mr. Branson for a moment or two.

Susan left the kitchen, passed through the lightless living room, and pressed her face against the front door. She looked through the door peep onto the lit front porch.

Outside stood Tanuki. No, even if it wore the face of their beloved cat, it couldn't be. *It couldn't. . . not Tanuki, not with his head on the body of a boy.*

The boy's body was bookish and pale, just as Susan always imagined Tanuki.

Tanuki held a platter of meat. All seven of the daycare children stood around him.

"Meow, can we come in now?" Tanuki

said. He spoke in the voice of a six-year-old boy with a sore throat.

Susan threw the door open. She looked into the eyes of her dead cat and saw her husband approaching from behind.

Two hands wrapped around her belly.

"It's just me," said her husband. "Don't tense up like that."

She wanted to run away, but there was nowhere to go. Her husband kissed the back of her neck. "What's the matter with you?" he said.

"Nothing."

"Nothing? If nothing's the matter with you, then why the hell are you letting our guests sit outside in the cold? Ask them in for dinner.

"Go on," he said.

She looked at Tanuki and the children. She said, "Would you like to come in for dinner?"

Her husband jerked her inside and waved for Tanuki and the kids to follow. "Tanuki," he said gruffly, "take the kids into the kitchen. I'd like to speak with my wife alone."

Tanuki gave a thumbs up and shuffled into the kitchen. The children followed close behind, as if they feared passing beyond Tanuki's supervision.

Susan was bawling now. Hysterical, even. She was so ashamed of herself, to lose her composure like this. "What the hell's going on?" she said.

Her husband said, "Don't get upset over this. You've got no goddamn reason to get upset. I should slap the shit out of you. I *know* you've wanted us to start our own family for a while now and talking things with Ted, I said let's do it. Let's start our own family. We needed more money, but Ted said just have a few extra workers. Kids will pay for kids. Ted told me how. I invited him to live with us."

"Slow down," Susan said, starting to gain her composure. "Slow down. Where did you meet Ted? Why did he come here this morning?"

"How did I meet who? Who did I meet?"

"Ted Branson. How did you meet Ted Branson?"

Her husband crossed his arms and head-butted her like a wooden Indian chief. "I met him nowhere special," he said.

Susan buckled over. She pulled her hair. She clawed at her husband's feet. *This is it*, she thought, *I've done it for sure. This knitted little life of mine is gone for good.* "Nowhere special," she sobbed, "nowhere special. For God's sake, what does that mean? Nowhere spe—"

He kicked a dirty Reebok into her *chomp-chomps*, as he had nicknamed the cat's teeth.

She bit her tongue and it burst in half.

"I didn't mean that," her husband said, as Susan gagged up blood.

"Truly, I didn't. All I want is for you to understand that we can finally start a family. I want *you* to be happy. *We* can finally be happy. And if it's really that important to you, I met Ted in a bathroom. He was looking for a daycare service."

Susan looked up at her husband. Was this really her husband? She had always considered him the more rational of the two of them, and while she knew *she* was being irrational, well, he had was an abusive spouse!

But then she thought of Tanuki's death, and it hurt far worse than everything he had just done to her.

"Where did Tanuki come from?" she said.

"That's mine and Ted's business," he said.

"Ted and I decided that since Tanuki might have trouble acquiring a job, he's the best candidate for fatherhood. Ted and I will provide financial support while you stay home with Tanuki and the kids. We'll be the perfect family."

In the kitchen, Tanuki's mewing laughter pitched above the kid laughter. *This is not my life*, she thought. *I cannot be Susan. Make me into someone else. I cannot be Susan. I have always been just Susan. Please. Anyone. Make. Me. Into. Someone Else. Anyone. Or someone, come here to me.*

Despite the transformations of her world, she remained stifled, obedient, and afraid. In other words, she remained painfully herself.

Everything grew quiet. Her partially-severed tongue hung over her bottom lip. She let the blood run down her chin.

"It's dinner time," her husband said, standing at the front of the table, but Ted was not out with the dinner yet.

Susan leaned back in the seat opposite end her husband. She looked around at all the fleshless faces. Susan didn't want a family, or maybe she did still want one. Maybe she wanted this one. She didn't know. Nobody knew if they truly belonged to their family because nobody ever chose their family. She still loved her husband, she supposed. Susan also loved Tanuki.

"Dinner's not ready yet," Mr. Branson—Ted—called from the bathroom.

"Is he preparing dinner in the bathroom?" Susan asked. Forming each word hurt.

Tanuki whined about dinner taking too longer. Susan's husband told the cat-child that Father Ted would be just a minute. "He is preparing dinner right now," he said.

"What would it be like," she said, "to be in a family I chose to love?"

"You should ask Ted about that one. He's into Hallmark cards."

The children were laughing, but everyone stopped chattering as Ted stepped out of the bathroom carrying a silver platter holding a large rib-eye steak.

"I would like to bless this meal," Ted said. "Bow your heads, everyone."

Susan bowed her head. Ted began a prayer to the meat. *Lord Meat, we thank you for your sacrifice, for transforming our children so that someday we might also come to wear the perfect likeness of you . . .*

Susan wondered how long her tongue would bleed, and whether, exactly, the hanging part would interfere with her enjoyment of tonight's family dinner.

And, oh, the parents. WHAT ABOUT THE PARENTS? If anything, grown-up concerns are even more convoluted than the unmitigated weirdness of childhood.

As Nicole says, "This is a story about how people in general (and governments in particular) really don't make anything better, but convince everyone—including themselves—that they have by just changing the appearance of the problem. Deception, and self-deception."

Nicole Cushing has a knack for re-raveling our tattered cultural frameworks, in wrenching terms that yank the mind. At least they yank mine. Hang on to yours tight!

The Bureaucratic Nativity of Panda Christ
by Nicole Cushing

Blessed are the Peace Keepers, for They shall be called sons of the gods.
—Jesus, The Sermon on the Mount (Matthew 5:9), New Galactic Peace Version (2073)

The bald Anglo wore a Peace sign on his lapel and wobbled into the maternity suite brandishing a pistol, a briefcase, and a smile. He groaned, then let the briefcase slide off his fingers. It smacked the faux-wooden floor, triggering a fragile, shrill howl from Karen's newborn. The bald man said something she couldn't quite make out over her baby boy's crying, but the parts she could decipher chilled her to the bone. No, she couldn't have heard the man right—she'd gotten a license to deliver this child, active case of vitiligo or not. The rhythm of her heart monitor quickened.

The man leaned over her and flashed a badge. He spoke loud enough to be heard over the crying. A little too loud. "I'll be taking the baby now, official Peace business," he hollered. The words came out with a sing-song slurring. The scent of liquor wafted in the wake of his breath. His shaking hand kept the gun trained in the general vicinity of Karen's splotchy, clownish face.

Karen wept and clung the infant to her breast. She didn't say a word.

The Government Drunk looked at Karen wide-eyed, then paused and rattled off some phrases. "Habla Usted Espanol?" he asked. "Ni huo shuo Zhongwen ma?"

Karen understood just enough Spanish and Mandarin to get into trouble. Even the smattering she knew helped, given that people attributed all sorts of ethnic identities to her. Her affliction guaranteed it. Despite being born with a rich, mahogany hue, the vitiligo gobbled up her dark pigment in a semi-regular, symmetrical pattern—leaving only oases of blackness around her eyes and ears. The rest looked white as an Anglo in January. The more ballsy strangers came up and asked to have photos taken with her. Some people assumed she was a body mod geek, and she found herself approached too many times by college kids with filed-fang teeth and tattooed scales who asked where she'd had her permanent make-up done. They called her The Panda Girl, and told her that they meant it as a compliment. After getting to know her, they said they considered her fortunate to have "achieved by virtue of disease" a resemblance to something animal—a type of appearance which they had obtained only through great time and expense.

But most people (or at least most *decent* people) avoided her. Only the gods knew why. Vitiligo wasn't contagious. It was genetic, with perhaps some environmental influence. Her baby boy, for example, was brown enough now, but over the years might well lose his pigment just as she had. But even though it wasn't contagious, she was used to the confusion: about vitiligo, of course, but even more so about *her*. "What are you?" was a question shot her way more than once.

The Government Man stared at her face, as if trying to take in an inkblot. "Unazungumza Kiswahili?" he asked, this time with a lilt in his voice. Karen could tell that this time he'd thought he'd finally nailed it.

"I only speak English," she said.

"Then you heard what I said the first time," the Government Drunk huffed. "I'll be taking the baby now."

Instead, Karen clung her seven-pound newborn all the closer to her breast. She pushed the button to call a nurse. None came. Only the trappings of authority—the wallet-badge, the Peace sign on his lapel—prevented her from joining her son in a scream-fest.

A trail of badge-and-taser types filtered in the room after the drunk Government Man. A Sheriff's deputy. Some rent-a-cop hospital security. Outgunned and outnumbered, she felt herself recede into the hospital bed. She wanted once more to envelop her baby. "Put him back in!" she almost-said. He'd been safe there, inside her. Now less than an hour after she evicted him from within her, the Government Man wanted to take him even further. Where, she did not know.

All she did know was that the Government Drunk wasn't shooting her as long as she held what he wanted.

"It's a matter of world Peace," he said.

"I don't care," Karen said. Her teeth gritted with the same determination that had gotten her through labor. "So I have a skin problem, that's not enough to take away a child!"

"That skin *condition* is part of the reason we *must* take him away, Ma'am. Now, the baby please." The man's pistol hand shook, and with his free hand he removed a tiny bottle of whiskey from his suit pocket, unscrewed the cap with two nimble fingers, gulped it down, and tossed it into a receptacle intended for medical waste.

Karen scanned the room for allies. The World Peace Agency had its foes. Rumors abounded of local, state, and national law enforcement bristling at the Worldies coming in and assuming jurisdiction. Perhaps she could divide and conquer. She looked at the Deputy, then back to the Government Man. "Taking kids away isn't Peace Agency business. I think you're meddling in a local matter."

The bald man swept his hand over his gleaming head and coughed. "I hate to drop their name unless I really have to," the Drunk mumbled. "But it's all about the Peace Keepers." He giggled and snorted. The Deputy and hospital security wrung their hands. They looked back and forth between Karen and the drunk Government Man.

A sense of dread descended over the room like a fog. Karen felt that she was in way over her head. She guessed that everyone else did, too. No one on Earth could even pronounce the name of the Peace Keepers' planet, let alone face Them on anything like an equal footing. All anyone knew was that They were —by writ of a Galactic Magistrate—the new custodians of all non-human life on Earth, and would be until that same Magistrate decided this filthy boondock-world could handle autonomy again. It was as if the entire planet had been placed on a type of probation, and the Government Drunk had just announced the fate of each of Earth's billions of creatures rested, inscrutably, on a lumpy-headed infant who'd not even yet moved his bowels for the first time. The whole room suddenly looked red and sweaty.

"Correction!" he bellowed, perhaps picking up the cues that his disclosure stirred more anxiety than it quelled "it has absolutely nuthin' to do with no Peace Keepers! Is that understood?"

In vino veritas, Karen thought, convinced that the Government Drunk had let the truth slip and then made a poor attempt to cover up the confirmation. She saw beads of sweat on his forehead . His pupils were too big and too black. She was the one who'd just given birth, she was the one asked to surrender her child. Yet somehow, since uttering the name "Peace Keepers," the Government Man looked even more clammy, more ill, more nervous than she. *He's a drunken fool*, Karen thought, *but no one will stand in his way. Not with his Masters involved.*

Indeed, he was the one with the badge. He was the one in charge. He was the one even then twirling the pistol around his clumsy fingers, like a twelve year old aspiring gunslinger.

Karen looked at the Deputy, who dodged her gaze and looked at his shoes. She looked at the Drunk with the gun. "What do the Peace Keepers want with my baby?"

The sergeant stepped forward. "Sir, I've been a cop here since '37. I remember a world without Peace Keepers. If they're the reason you need to take this infant from its mother—"

"*His* mother," Karen interrupted. "He's not an 'it', he's a person."

The cop nodded. "If They're the reason you need to take this infant from *his* mother, I'm not fool enough to try to stop you. But I think the lady at least deserves an explanation."

The Government Man sighed and shook his head "Due pwow-cess," he lisped. "Okay, okay. I'm *realllly* not supposed to tell you about this." He put his index finger in front of his lips. "Shhhhhh" he said, then burst into a giggle. Karen could see the Government Man was trying to restrain a monumental gut buster, but was losing the battle. He let out a raucous titter. "It's a see-quit."

The cop glared at him. "You show up in my town. Drunk. By the look of your eyes, probably high, too. Demanding to take away Miss Young's son. You're going to tell us all what this is about, or else I'll call the W.P.A. and tell them one of their errand boys showed up toasted."

The Government Man paused, as if momentarily sobered up by the threat. "You have a point. Yes, I do owe her that much. You see, it's all about the pandas."

The Government Drunk had to be insane. Karen pushed the button to summon the nurses again—two, three, four times. She bit her lip.

"We're . . . um . . . short a few pandas," the Government Man said. Then he cleared his throat.

Karen looked up from the button. She heard herself and a few others gasp.

"And the Peace Keepers are coming, you see. A semi-surprise inspection, they called it, in just a few days. And, well, you can understand our dismay, after everything they threatened to do last time. Of course, we hear that it's the Magistrate on Gilese who has final say on these things—not that you'd know it by the way those Peace Keepers talk."

"They're terminating our rights?" the cop asked.

Karen's stomach, still reeling from the extended fast required by induced labor, did somersaults when she heard the cop point out the possibility of Earth being found guilty of biosphere neglect.

The Government Man smiled. "Exterminating, er, terminating our rights?" he said, a bit too loudly. "Cào nǐ māde!"

Karen couldn't piece together a complete translation, but she was pretty sure the Government Drunk just said something filthy. He disgusted her.

"How can you be so flip?" she snarled. "And what does this have to do with my son?"

"If the Peace Keepers pick up on the panda shortage," the Government Drunk slurred, "they'll find Earth non-compliant with The Agreement, right?"

Karen nodded.

The Government Drunk tapped one of his wingtips against the floor. "And if found non-compliant with The Agreement, homo sapiens would be found guilty of biosphere neglect, right?"

Karen nodded.

"And if found guilty of biosphere neglect, the Peace Keepers would transport all of the animals to a . . ." he paused for effect, waved the gun around, and took on the persona of a high school teacher quizzing a class. "Anyone?"

"A foster planet," Karen croaked.

"Yep. Imagine every single animal—all of them—gone. Every honey bee, every cow, every hoof of pork and wing of poultry."

"We'd all be going vegetarian," the Deputy said.

The Government Drunk glared at the Deputy. "There wouldn't be any veggies to tarry-on, you dolt! No bees to pollinate, no cow poop to fertilize. Hell, if the Peace Keepers had their way, they wouldn't even leave behind any bacteria to break poop down into fertilizer!"

"We'd have our own poop," one of the hospital security guards said. "The whole world wouldn't be poop-less."

Karen felt ill, and dry heaved. She punched the emergency call button with a manic energy she'd not thought she'd possess after all she'd been through today. Still, no nurse came.

She swallowed a trickle of bile that found its way up her throat. "I just delivered a baby. Do you *mind*? You've upset me and my son long enough. All of this might be important, but it has nothing to do with us. I'm going to ask you to leave, and ask the hospital security to escort you, Sir."

In her heart, she knew she was bluffing, and knew that one way or another the Government Man was driving at some chain-of-reasoning that ended with taking away her son. Karen looked at her baby boy. Assuming the drunk Government Man's panda shortage wasn't just some three-sheets-to-the-wind psychosis, the whole planet was in for a bleak future. But the planet could go to Hell for all she cared. Her son, in particular, was all that mattered. If all animals were taken to a foster planet, he'd starve before he turned three. She might not last much longer. She grew pale.

The Government Man tucked his glistening hand in his jacket pocket and whipped out a green-and-white document. The motion swept him too far forward, and he nearly tumbled onto Karen and the baby. The whole room winced until hospital security steadied him. He dropped the heavy legal pronouncement onto the bed. Karen unfolded it with one hand, still cradling her infant in the opposite arm. Black bold lettering ran across the top of the document: ORDER OF SPECIES RECLASSIFICATION. A foil seal, adorned with ribbon, had been stuck to the bottom right corner.

Then the Government Man smirked.

"Miss Young," He couldn't contain himself. He made snorting, whinnying giggles. "Your child will save us. New challenges demands a new Christ, I think you'll agree. This tyke is up to the task. A federal judge just ruled. He isn't a boy—he's um, a panda."

Karen gritted her teeth. Her heart sank. "Just because we have vitiligo doesn't make us pandas! People have called me names all my life because of this, and now you bastards hurt my son the same way. What's the point?"

The Government Man cackled. "Ms. Young, please, I think you misunderstand. There's no insult implied." More slurring. "It's just that the Whirled Peas Council . . ." More laughter. "They just passed Public Law XRQ-25-25, 50-92 40-77"

"What?" the cop said.

"The Species Reclassification Act. It's a—It's a—" Then he whinnied some more, cackled so hard he cried.

The Deputy gasped. Karen saw his brow crinkle as he connected the dots.

"Loophole," the cop sighed. "It's a loophole."

"On the nose!" the Drunk yelled, planting his right index finger just below his left eye socket. "The Peace Makers said that we could pass any ol' law we wanted to take care of the biosphere. And we needed a bigger panda population, and a smaller human population, and your O.B.'s second-trimester genetic tests suggest that your son is 97% likely to inherit not only vitiligo itself, but your unique panda-pattern-vitiligo in particular. So you see, it only made sense: we have expanded the legal definition of 'panda' to include homo sapiens with panda-like appearance and qualities! Call it type-casting!"

"Type casting?" one of the security guards quipped, "call it a *miracle*! No more panda shortage!" The guard applauded, and it soon became contagious. "Quick thinkin'!" another guard said. "Crisis averted!" whooped the Deputy.

"Wait!" Karen said. "In spite of my . . . our . . . skin disease my son is *not* a panda! He's a human boy, the same as any other – look, do you really think the Peace Keepers are going to be fooled?"

"He is *too* a panda," the Government Drunk whined, sounding a bit hurt. "He's a panda in the most important sense: the legal sense. He's the world's first *paperwork* panda. But don't worry he'll look more the part in a sec." He found his briefcase half-obscured under Karen's hospital bed. He fidgeted with it for several seconds, and Karen heard the clicking of buttons as he entered a combination. He hoisted a small piece of black-and-white cloth in the air.

"Behold! Swaddling cloths fit for a King! Through your Son, the End shall be prevented! Through your Son, our whole planet shall be saved!"

"Jesus Christ!" Karen said. " That's not 'swaddling cloths', it's a panda costume!"

"Bien sur!" the Government Man said. The dude must've liked showing off his languages when he got trashed. "It's a little big," the Drunk continued, sounding oddly mothering, "but he'll grow into it." He tossed the costume onto the bed. "I'm sure you can understand the need to not only look panda-esque in the face, but all over his body. It will increase his odds of bonding with a panda mother and a whole panda herd—or flock, or whatever—once he's out there, all alone, in the wild. And now that I've taken the time to explain myself, I must demand the baby." He pointed the pistol at Karen. "I don't want to kill you, Mother Mary, but I will if it's the only way to bring Salvation."

The Government Man was grinning.

It was clear, the Government Man's patience was waning. He'd explained it all. She could try to keep her newborn, and likely die in the process. And even if she somehow succeeded—which would require either the cop or some of the hospital security to defect to her side—she'd have to contend with a world without other animals, or even fertilizer. A world of starvation, or even worse, cannibalism.

Tears slid down her cheeks. "I want to go with him. Make me a panda, too."

The Government Man clutched the gun to his heart as if it were a dozen roses. "Mother Mary, selfless Mary! Bearer of the Savior! We have a suit just in your size." He slurred each successive "s." "I brought it with me just hoping that you'd come to see things my way. One less person, one more panda! Oh, the Peace Keepers will be thrilled. I'll have the paperwork drawn up post-haste, then we'll be flying you to a bamboo forest in Sichuan Province. Perhaps there you'll find the cub a father, eh?" The Government man smiled.

That last line hurt. Her son *had* a father. He just ran when he'd heard he'd impregnated a "freak."

But lo, there appeared, wriggling through the gaggle of hospital security three nurses, bearing white gift bags stuffed with black tissue paper. One bag was small, one bag huge, with a third bag of medium size. A tall brunette carrying the biggest bag spoke first. "We saw your emergency call signal lighting up our board like a Christmas tree, but we understood you had, um, a visitor." She glanced at the Drunk. "He left these behind at the nurse's station."

The Government Man chuckled. "How silly of me. I'd forgotten." He looked down at his pistol, and gave it a playful waggle. "I'd simply . . . run out of hands on my way in, you

see. Thank you kind ladies for remembering. Could you please present the W.P.A.'s parting gifts to Madonna and Child?"

"We couldn't help but overhear this good news" a short round blonde said. "for unto us, a panda is born! We'd be honored to present him these gifts."

Then Karen saw it. The three nurses knelt on the floor in front of her. The Government Drunk had been right—she'd misunderstood. There'd been no insult implied in re-classifying her son (and luckily, herself as well) as the world's first paperwork pandas. No insult at all. Before all of this, her vitiligo made the world despise her, reject her. But now, given this unanticipated turn of events, she found herself and her son being worshiped. Every dog—every *panda*—has its day, and this day belonged to her and her Son.

The nurses raised their gift bags on high. She opened the smallest first, and found nestled in the black tissue paper a rattle shaped like a tasty stalk of bamboo. The largest bag held a baby-sling, which she could use to tote her son close to her chest. It'd be essential in the wild, since she'd be crawling on all fours. The final gift was a set of three cloth diapers. She'd use them during the long plane trip, but would probably discard them afterward. They were too much of a human artifact, far too human for a proper panda. *But they were symbolic*, she thought, *a reminder that, through the saving work of her Son, the Earth would not want for poop.*

Yes, it was the gods' will. It was the government's will. It was the government's gods' will. She gave her newborn son to the Drunk, and hummed *Ave Maria,* savoring its words in the deepest recess of her spirit.

For behold, from henceforth: all generations shall call me blessed.

The United Kingdom has for centuries been a profound repository of distinctive strangeness, with such proto-Bizarros as Jonathan Swift, Lewis Carroll, and Monty Python's Flying Circus leaping straight off the tip of my iceberg, just for starters.

Representing the U.K. Weirdness Team this go-round is veteran purveyor D. F. Lewis, who had published no less than 1,500 short fictions before this century even began.

Des tells me, "I wrote "The Perfect Pitch Of Reality" in the nineteen-eighties, in retrocausality from a bad toilet day in old age during the 20th century." And you'll believe him, too, as he reveals at last the nature of the shit that underlies all creation.

The Perfect Pitch of Reality
by D. F. Lewis

When Sir Padgett Weggs looked at himself in the mirror, he discovered that he was not the person he thought he was. The other Knight in the Mess came running over, on hearing him scream out.

"What be the trouble, young Padgett? You sound as if the Devil himself has taken berth in your very soul!" said Sir Blasphemy Fitzworth, his voice staying caln but betraying a hint of concern for his lifelong companion.

Whilst Sir Padgett was a surly character, with worry lines fanning in every direction across his 'chamberpot' of a face, Sir Blasphemy was a more typical Knight of the Cousinship, with lips turned up at the corners, in contrast to the droop-fish versions swimming across the other's face. Sir Padgett's eyes, too, were pitted, whilst those of Sir Blasphemy were usually receptive to the busybodying reflections of the stars aloft . . .

"Come, come, Sir Padgett Weggs, as I have learned to call you," said Sir Blasphemy, "This is no time for self-pity. We've a Trial and a Quest to keep in motion."

"I know, I know, but I'm riven with self-doubt." Sir Padgett continued to stare into the mirror, wondering which was the image and which the image maker. He could hear the cranking and churning of the pump outside, no doubt being tended by the other Knights . . . there would be Sir Sinecure Wabbit looking over the dials and also ensuring that the mighty pump retained sufficient lubrications in its moving parts; a dear man, Sir Sinecure; also, Sir Ervin Tourner, the only Knight among them who actually dressed up like one, in full armoured leggings and coat of arms; he would be preening himself, stroking his cockade as if it were a living tissue, a vibrant issue of his thews . . .

Sir Stripling Welham mopped his brow. He looked askance at the other Knights who had rushed out from the Mess in a bit of a tiswas but they couldn't be blamed for thinking the worst, the pump was spluttering like mad and throwing up bits of brown sludge like fartfire into the dawn sky; the pistons were going two to the dozen, their sumpsucks drying up on the attenuating layers of nightsoil that Sir Stripling thought the earth incubated . . .

This was his lock, stock and barrel; his whole lifeforce depended on the mining of Earthclosets pocketed like wind bubbles throughout the underfeet lands; he would live off selling the opulent effluent that the pump had been designed to syphon. The other Knights of the Cousinship were just pawns in a game controlled by a cheating dungeonmaster God, all seeds in Sir Stripling's search for the one cache of gruel, the rarest spadeoak of stiffened slurry, the sole grail of bowelfodder, which would make a mint for him to get through the Bad Times; but, give him his due, after his needs were satisfied, then the other Knights would be allowed to fight over the rest.

Sir Padgett Weggs was left alone in
the Mess. He was Knight pure and true. He looked again into the mirror and he in the mirror looked back, and both were surprised to see the tears in the other's eyes. His illusions were about to be shattered. All the Knights, he included, had passed the Test of Wisdom, the Trial of Initiation, crawled on hands and knees through dark dripping burrows and emerged finally from a cave where an incontinent Dragon had been said to leave its defecations as well as remnants of its brimstone … and, on emerging, the drops of stench- fruit would fall away from their flesh, leaving it as unblemished as a virgin's breast (for all virgins have nippleless breasts).

Once marked with the Cruciform at Cousinship, the Knights were not allowed to produce a single tangled turd from between their lower cheeks. So fasting in this way … living just for the everonward Trial and Quest at Existence without Throughput, the Knights just drifted through the endless empathies that Big Pump supplied, and taught themselves to be merely content with such surrogates that spilt from Earth's innards.

Sir Padgett's tears were shed on behalf of the Cousinship. Sir Stripling had evidently let them all down—so the mirror said. All the Knights, bar one, believed that their Godgiven task, whilst here on Earth, was one of fighting on Spirit's behalf against Spirit's inevitable incarnate stirrings. But that one other Knight fought equally hard for those very stirrings, gaining a Hero's Force from staring into hot brown springs, glorying in gory geysers, almost for their very own sake; relishing all the riches he fancied he could get from marketing saunas of steaming manpats, jacuzzis of bubbling decomposition . . .

Sir Padgett decided to take things into his own hands. He unoathed his oaths, unvowed his vows; he unlaced his trews, squinted at the hairy hindparts in the mirror and squeezed a tiny turd upon its shining, disgusted surface. It crawled upon it like a slug, smearing and slurring the perfect pitch of reality that the mirror had heretofore contained.

The Knights of the Cousinship knelt
around the dead pump, deep in unthinking prayer. Sir Padgett had by now joined them, his forehead resting on the ground, as if the Earth and he were one, only divided by the thinness of a skull. Sir Sinecure, Sir Ervin and Sir Blasphemy had just discovered that unthinking prayer is no better than death, their nostrils snot-ended, their lips double-gummed with slick substance that had found the easiest exit.

Sir Stripling was head down in the shitpump's silent silo, looking for the cheating God Who had already disappeared to his Dungeon of Dung.

It's hard to do new things with old monsters. Especially vampires: the ultimate pop standards, so conspicuously overexposed that you wonder why they haven't all died from the never-ending light shone upon them.

But Amelia excels at upgrading mythological software: sexually transmitted zombies, just for starters. And as she was quick to point out, when I expressed my reservations, "I don't care much for them, either; that's part of the challenge!

"Vampires have this reputation of being preternaturally calm and resourceful," she continued, "but this feels very much at odds with the amount of blood they spill." And from there flows this utterly punk rock story, full of laughs and weirdness and surprising soul.

Rough Music
by Amelia Beamer

They'd been drunk when they came up with The Plan: the kind of drunk you can only get with your band mates. It was a really good plan, The Plan. Battle of the Bands was coming up at The Derby, and Monkeyfist had been racking their collective brains to come up with something new. Their "Baby Doll Rape" set last year had gotten them third place, which was great, except that ever since, Anonymous Ed went limp whenever he was fucking a girl and her eyes rolled back in her head.

But this year's Plan would make last year's show look like warm beer. This would be so much awesome they'd have to clean it up with a mop.

Except when Anonymous Ed woke the next night, the details of The Plan had turned to hot urine. These band mates were the best that he'd ever had, so he must have gotten pretty drunk. His head pulsated with pain: this wasn't fair. Vampires weren't supposed to get hangovers.

He sweated in his sheets until it was time for practice, then rushed through his routine morning stab at cleanliness, changing into his last clean pair of pants and his "College" T-shirt, and helping himself to somebody's blood stash in the refrigerator, aptly named Hair of the Dog. Just enough to clear his head. His housemates knew you had to label your shit, or else it was free game.

He was downstairs in the studio, tuning his guitar in the dark and thinking about possible song titles—"Tuning in the Dark?"—when Amber Dextrous showed up, tweaked out and smelling of burned marshmallows. Anonymous Ed loved Amber Dextrous with the kind of love that made trouble. You were never supposed to fall in love with your band mates, particularly if they were hotter than you. And Amber Dextrous was an eighth-grader at the senior prom kind of hot, which mostly made up for the fact that she wasn't a very good bass player, and had a voice like a fish. Monkeyfist was a rebound band for her, and she stuck around, Anonymous Ed thought, mostly for the attention.

She turned on the fan and the light, and lit a cigarette. "How you doing, punkin'?" she asked.

"Good," Anonymous Ed lied. "Actually, it was a rough day. Kept waking up shaking. Nightmares, you know?" This was also a lie; the drink had knocked him out cold, but he and Amber Dextrous always bonded over their shared symptoms.

"Jesus boned a hooker, tell me about it," Amber Dextrous said. "I couldn't sleep, so I went running. Was supposed to go to my group therapy after sunset, but the idea of sitting around with those losers, talking about shit that happened to us decades ago . . . Sometimes I just want to tell them all to get the fuck over it already."

Smoke drifted up between her glasses and her eyes. Anonymous Ed didn't feel too bad manipulating her because she was manipulative, too: she wore those glasses just to get the geek guys to love her. Instead of Bentleys, they brought her Ataris and T-shirts with clever slogans. Still, they let her bite them, and they were usually pretty clean.

Anonymous Ed had taken her sloppy seconds, more than once—virgin boys whose blood tasted of Doritos and Mountain Dew—although he wouldn't like to admit it. Not that he was homophobic: he just liked to seduce people himself.

"I know?" Anonymous Ed said. "It's pretty freaking inevitable that *everyone* will get PTSD, especially people who've lived as long as us." He caught the look she gave him. "I still maintain that we *are* people. We've just done more shit, and we've had more shit done to us."

Amber Dextrous made a dismissive, feminine gesture that was her way of telling him to fuck off. She was younger than him, and newer at being undead. Not that it made much difference if you were within a few decades. He wanted to pull her into his lap, but knew he'd have to get her blood-drunk first.

He decided to make himself sound sensitive. "I was dreaming about the night it happened. Did I ever tell you that I'd secretly wanted to be turned? I'd look on Craigslist for the vamps who were looking for 'companions' —I thought it'd be romantic." He remembered that chicks dug guy-on-guy action, or at least foreplay.

"Ew. Seriously?" She put out her cigarette in an empty mug. "That's such a high-school idea of *romantic*. So are you still down for The Plan?" Her eyes got larger, and she smiled.

"Um, yeah, of course," Anonymous Ed said. He put in his earplugs. Used to be, his whole body would shake for an hour or more when he finished a gig, or even a practice set. He'd asked Dr. Google, and found that psychogenic tremors were common. So was hypervigilance—if he didn't put in his earplugs, too much sound came into his brain, and his body would freak out. Earplugs also provided a convenient excuse for when he occasionally misunderstood people.

"The Plan," he repeated. "What's wrong with The Plan?"

Amber Dextrous smiled that half-smile that drove the Mountain Dew crowd out of their shorts. "Are you really going to stake Down Pat onstage tonight?"

"No, Pat, no!" Anonymous Ed said. When he got flummoxed, he channeled Dr. Seuss. This would have made him a really good uncle, except he didn't have any nieces and nephews.

"Yeah, I know. It was his idea," Amber Dextrous said.

"Fucking-A," Anonymous Ed said. He thought he'd heard her say that The Plan was to stake Down Pat, their suicidal drummer. But that was a horrible idea. She must have said "fake" or "make" or "bake." Shake and bake? He ran through possible words in his head. His guitar wasn't getting any more tuned. "Strap up and plug in already, babe, he'll be here in a minute," Anonymous Ed said, irritated with himself. He hated forgetting things. It made him feel old.

"Down Pat said not to talk about it with him," Amber Dextrous said from behind the fortress of her bass. "In case he changed his mind."

Anonymous Ed turned up the volume, and ignored the way his hands started shaking when Down Pat showed up a few minutes later. Down Pat was smiling like the Virgin Mary who got into the cream.

The competition started around midnight, which was early for this crowd, but there were a lot of bands to get through. Monkeyfist sat at the bar, nursing their drinks and avoiding eye contact with one another. Chicks with Bricks had brought poi spinners: leathery-muscled women who slung chains of fire in a way that looked terribly easy as they danced through the crowd. They christened the evening with the first casualty, setting a long-haired drunk on fire. The emergency crew was perfect, sirens in tune with the set, and so well timed that Anonymous Ed suspected it was an inside job. It was an old-fashioned, almost classic trick, blood on the stage. The crowd loved it, and even the EMTs were bobbing their heads.

Anonymous Ed pressed his leg against Amber Dextrous's. "Smoke. Outside," he said. That was one thing he'd always liked about smoking: it was always an excuse to be alone without anyone checking on you. Not that he really had the kind of friends who would check on each other.

They joined the mass exodus of people also going outside to smoke between sets.

Anonymous Ed walked up the street. When they were semi-alone, he took out his earplugs and said: "So what's The Plan for tonight?" He pretended they'd never talked about it.

"You're going to stab Down Pat, on stage." She used her Talking to Retards voice. "Like we talked about. Or I swear, I'm 'a stab you."

Anonymous Ed was pretty sure he'd misheard her, so he put his earplugs back in. "You said I'm going to grab Down Pat. Then you're going to grab me. How is that a show? Last year we had hella props, and this year we don't have anything." Monkeyfist was supposed to be *his* band. He wasn't sure how he'd let Amber Dextrous take charge. He must be losing his shit.

Amber Dextrous put a hand on Anonymous Ed's chest, right where his heart should be. He'd donated it, once he didn't need it any more; it had been the fashionable thing to do, back in the day. He used to make jokes about it. He put his hand over hers, and searched her eyes.

"I love you," he said. "If someone has to die tonight, it should be me." He didn't try to hide his shaking. He didn't want to kill Down Pat just for a rock show.

"I love you," she said. Or maybe she said, "Fuck you." She turned, and he followed. They were going to miss Itchy Startled Wet.

Anonymous Ed did his breathing exercises while the bands played. He closed his eyes through I Hate Myself And I Want To Die, a 30-piece marching band from Pomona who did their set piece with chickens. Then there was Pastor Bible Belt, which had a real ex-pastor, and a real belt; they'd added a nun choir since he'd seen them last. Anonymous Ed opened his eyes at one point to see the lead singer from Beggars and Choosers strung upside-down, flaying her belly with a knife. Thick pink scars covered her body.

Anonymous Ed had a headache by now, and the shaking in his hands hadn't stopped even though he'd taken his medication. Strobe lights played over the crowd, a fragmented buzz of freeze frames, everyone in mid-jump. He suspected the crowdsurfing had gone bad already. The EMTs came and went, stretchering out band members and trampled crowd. The EMTs weren't dancing any more.

Monkeyfist was going on soon. Anonymous Ed ought to stand up. "Tweetle beetle puddle battle!" he said. His headache had blossomed into a full-blown migraine, and as the nausea hit, Anonymous Ed came to understand something. Something important. Music wasn't just about making a violent spectacle. The EMTs, they saw violence all the time, and they weren't entertained by the violence tonight. It was the *music* that had made them nod their heads. He needed to tell Amber Dextrous. They could stand out just by playing their music.

They had to move fast to set up. There was no time to tell Amber Dextrous. Anonymous Ed shouldered his guitar and decided to talk to the crowd instead. He felt a twinge of stage fright, and then it disappeared. He wasn't sure what he was going to say until he heard his voice in the monitor.

"I love blood as much as anyone here," he said. "But I want to confess something. I used to be an EMT, before I took up music and drinking blood. And it took me years to understand what had happened to me, because I thought I was fine. It's only after you get out of the violence when you start getting the flashbacks, and the shaking, and the headaches. Anyone here been an EMT?"

The EMTs nodded. Anonymous Ed could feel his band mates staring at him, nervous and confused at where he might be going. You didn't alienate your audience, not if you wanted them to love you: everyone knew that.

Anonymous Ed kept talking. "You ever done CPR, mouth to mouth, and felt the guy die? You ever sat with the corpse in your wagon, not wanting to go back to the hospital because they'll only send you out again?"

The EMTs had stopped treating people and were looking at Anonymous Ed with tears in their eyes and blood on their gloves. The remaining crowd was restless, moving towards the bar, the bathroom, or the front door. Anonymous Ed didn't care if he lost them. They weren't ready to listen.

He realized something else. "You only get Post Traumatic Stress Disorder when you're out of the trauma. Stay inside the trauma, and you'll be OK." That was what everyone was here to do: distract themselves from their problems by reveling in those of others.

It was time to put on their show. He turned to Amber Dextrous. She was angry. He loved her even more for being angry. They played their opener, "Rats in the Walls," and then their current favorite, "Dental Damn." Amber Dextrous sung like a drowned ox, and Down Pat jammed like a man going off to war, and Anonymous Ed loved them both. He wanted this moment never to end.

Amber Dextrous caught Anonymous Ed's eye. She nodded at Down Pat. Anonymous Ed shook his head. Amber Dextrous hefted a drumstick, threatening. Anonymous Ed closed his eyes and played. Even without a heart to stab, a stake would kill him.

Monkeyfist launched into their closer, a wooden rollercoaster of a song called "Tease Me."

Anonymous Ed opened his eyes. The EMTs were dancing.

To me, the central question posed by most Bizarro fiction is the same one at the root of all philosophical inquiry: "What the fuck? You mean THIS is reality?" And few tales walk straight in as hard as this consensus-thwacking gem.

The only thing Kevin has to say about it is that no story has ever fought him harder. But I thought it was brilliant, so we wrestled it down. Sometimes beauty is worth every second of the struggle.

Enjoy this unhinged case in point.

Happiness is a Warm Gun
by Kevin L. Donihe

Today *will be a better day.*

Those words were in Bob's head as he awoke, even as veins in the ceiling pulsed and a dirty old grandfather clock swung a massive penis, once a pendulum, and leered lasciviously with twelve numbered eyes.

He tried not to think too much about this, or the alarm that attempted to seize his fingers with a crab's pinchers as he stretched, or the lamp that resembled a shaded sea cucumber and extended diaphanous filaments to snatch a fly. He couldn't change these things, but he could adapt to them. For too long, he'd carried himself like a thief in his own house, huddled up in closets or the bathtub, not eating, often naked, crying and screaming. It was time to prove that he was stronger than his possessions and live as best he could.

The first thing to do, Bob figured, was get dressed, as would a normal person on a normal morning. He arose, carpet fibers brushing willfully against his feet, tickling them.

The wardrobe was a swollen mushroom, but the dresser had been itself for two consecutive days, a minor miracle. He opened a drawer, reached down for his clothes, and a t-shirt reared up, flaring green and mossy sleeves. It wrapped around Bob's hand. He grabbed it, pulled. The thing wound tighter, but Bob tugged until there was enough in his hands to start ripping. On the floor, cotton fragments shook until they stilled.

I killed my shirt, he thought and wanted to cackle, but bit back the impulse. He'd given into it too often lately.

Instead, he regarded his other garments. Drawers brimmed with active clothing that would never stay on his body. Belts and ties slithered; dress shirts flapped and steamed; pants bubbled and oozed. All that remained unaltered were a pair of khaki shorts and navy blue briefs so old they might have been from his high school days. Bob winced as he pulled them over his hips.

Dressed, he walked into the hall past light fixtures like shrunken heads and into the living room where he tried to ignore the toadish armchair and the shrieking fireplace's yellow teeth. He was on his way to the kitchen, as the second thing one did on a normal morning was either eat or defecate. Shitting was out of the question; his bowels were empty.

It was crucial that the refrigerator be normal, not like yesterday when he was too cowed to use it. *Please, please, please . . .* he thought, an internal mantra. *Please, please, please.* But fists clenched; he stomped his feet. The fridge appeared as a huge, slumping block of cheese, riddled with holes that emitted plumes of steam.

Still, he reached for it, dreading the act, but imagining the food inside might still be edible. The handle was spongy. It pulsed in Bob's grip as he pulled.

Inside, a jug of orange juice sat on a rack once metal but now flesh. The jug scowled, its lid-mouth moving irregularly, angrily, sloshing oily black orange juice. A glassy pink worm, an ex-butter dish, swished a wilted broccoli tail; a bottle of dressing had swelled alongside an ancient meatloaf. The resulting fusion resembled a translucent puffer fish, studded in ground beef.

Bob closed the door. If he couldn't eat, then he could brush his teeth. He ran his tongue across them, felt grit and lumpy plaque.

On the way to the bathroom, he thought the words again, meant them, even as a drawer from the end table sprouted bat wings and flapped about the room:

Today will be a better day.

The toilet had transformed into a huge, rippling larynx. Bob took some perverse pleasure in urinating into it as it gurgled. Afterwards, he stood in front of the mirror and studied himself, his body so scrawny and disgusting, like something that might blow away with the wind or come up from the earth.

Looking down, he saw that the toothpaste tube was flat, and what little paste remained had hardened. He reached for the toothbrush. Its handle was red, wet, and corded, like an exposed muscle. Bristles were dirty brown, swaying slightly and thick as straw. They smelled like sulfur. No matter. He brought them to his mouth and scrubbed. Pain blossomed; he had to scream. The brush, he threw into the sink.

Bob looked at his shredded gums and at his red, clown-like smile. It wasn't the face of someone making a change in his life. It wasn't even the face of a sane man. He just walked away from the mirror, did not wipe the blood from his lips. There was no use.

Perhaps ending the day early was the only way to improve it.

Back in the bedroom, the penis clock still counted away the hours, but the lamp had become itself again. This didn't matter to Bob. He thought only of the rifle in the closet.

He threw open the door. A young, tow-headed woman sat where the firearm had, knees against her chest. She looked at him, but did not speak.

"Are you . . . the rifle?" he asked.

The woman nodded, though he couldn't tell if her answer had been yes or no. When she stood, Bob realized she was naked. Embarrassed, he looked past her, into the closet. The rifle definitely wasn't there.

As soon as the woman left the bedroom, a doorway in the hall became a jagged and enraged mouth, chomping incessantly. She continued toward it. Bob called out, covered his eyes, but the entryway stopped gnashing just before she passed beneath. He followed her warily, expecting the mouth to return and crush him.

The living room seemed upset that Bob's brains were not on the wall. Even wingless objects took flight, and the fireplace had dislodged itself to stumble around like a squat stone dwarf. Unfazed, the woman entered the room, and, one by one, flapping things lost their wings and fell to the floor. The fireplace's teeth retracted; it shot back into the wall. Shrunken heads became light bulbs.

Now, they sat at the kitchen table, Bob on one end, the woman on the other. Her hands rested on the table, long white fingers laced together. Her face—pale, oval—was expressionless. He just looked at her, trying to aim his stare at her eyes. They stared back at him, not offering a threat, just a puzzle. In front of her, everything was clean. Behind her, the refrigerator remained a lumpy monstrosity, leaning farther to the right, melting over and onto the stove, spreading its plague.

"I'm really hungry, so—uh—you don't suppose you could . . ."

She stood and granted his yet unspoken wish.

Bob hurried to the refrigerator. The interior was chilly, and food inside looked fresh, unmolested. He shoved slices of cheese, handfuls of cold cuts and meatloaf into his mouth; it didn't matter if things that should be warm weren't. He drank almost a full liter of cola, consumed three cups of chocolate pudding. It felt good to have something inside his stomach. For the first time in weeks, he felt solid, *tangible*.

He was so wrapped up in eating he almost forgot about the woman. Turning, he saw her watch him. "Sorry," he said, and wiped his mouth.

Satiated, Bob felt almost

clearheaded, and, after shaving and fixing his hair as best he could, devised a plan for the morning. He only hoped it would work.

The woman stood by a window, looking out, he imagined, at all the terrible things he couldn't bear to witness. He watched her for a few minutes, guiltily admiring the curves of her back, twiddling his fingers and biting his lip. Finally, he spoke.

"I wondered if . . . I mean, if you don't mind . . . I think I'd like to go out for a drive. Just a short one."

She turned from the window. This time he led, guiding her back to the bedroom where he put on shoes and a shirt and rummaged through newly restored clothing so she might have something to wear. Nothing was suitable, most of the garments too manly and wide, but he chose a pink button-up shirt, a pair of shorts matching his own and a belt to hold them.

She looked at the selection, shook her head.

"I know they're mine, but, if you go out, you're going to need some clothes."

She shook more adamantly.

He returned the clothes to the dresser. "Okay, I guess I can try to explain if we're pulled over."

At the front door, Bob paused. It had

been days since he'd tried to leave, and the last time hadn't been pleasant. He steeled himself, opened the door and peeked outside. Something black and shadowy whooshed down, nearly decapitating him. He drew himself back quickly. Through the window, he watched elastic tree branches smack at the porch, whipping side to side like angry men.

The woman grasped the knob. Bob fell back, and the tree ceased its thrashing as soon as she stepped outside.

He followed close behind her, looking out at the world that would have left him babbling had he been alone. The roofs of the neighboring houses were topped with weathered statues and gray gargoyles rather than antennae or chimneys. The houses themselves were brown and slouching; only one appeared normal. Below, grass was a fiery red. Above, clouds were grinning, gaseous things. Bob watched a bird fly into one and never reemerge.

The woman started down the porch. As she reached the last step, grass within a few feet of her became green. Clouds directly overhead: fluffy and white again.

In the driveway, the car was no longer a car, but a shaggy almost-dog with black matted fur, red headlights for eyes and a hideously extended exhaust pipe for a tail. Tires were studded with claws.

Bob pushed a button on the key ring, heard the sound of the door unlocking, and was amazed it still functioned. "I—I think you should get in the car first," he said, turning to the woman.

The moment before she touched the handle, a rudimentary arm, the beast became a late model Toyota, pale blue with rust spots.

Bob traveled through a world of change. It was only just outside the windshield where the status quo prevailed. Beyond, the road was a whipping serpent lined with natural and man-made atrocities, some entering the roadway as if to challenge the Toyota, only to return and transfigure when it approached them.

He glanced into the rearview mirror. For a few hundred yards, the backdrop seemed uncorrupted, but he noticed the bad things reestablishing themselves, filling in behind him like a wave moving at the speed of the car. He realized then that he was in a bubble.

The woman just looked out the window, hands together in her lap, something akin to a smile on her face.

"Thank you," he said. "I just wanted to say that."

The smile widened.

The Toyota entered the downtown area. While there might have been people amongst the rampaging buildings, automobiles, light posts and newspaper stands, it was hard to be sure. Every transformed thing was monstrous. Just ahead, a car was a sleek, black coffin on wheels. The driver, if it could be called as such, was a windswept skeleton, gray hair blowing on a bone scalp.

Bob drove around a park bounded by a circular intersection, curing the people and things around it, at least temporarily.

"I just want to sit here a few minutes," he said, pulling into a space by the park, "watch normal people do normal stuff."

And so he stared at people exiting and entering buildings, reading newspapers on benches, waiting for buses, and at construction men repairing pavement, police directing traffic past the work zone. The world remained ugly a few feet to the left of the park he'd circled, but people who entered the bubble became as themselves again, and things that shouldn't move were unable to cross.

"They don't know how good they have it," Bob said, shaking his head. He almost wanted to leave the car, wander about, but it seemed too early still. Even before the changes, the thought of interacting with a mass of humanity was nerve wracking. He reached for the ignition. "Okay, I've seen what I wanted to see. Let's go back."

The woman placed her hand over the keys.

"What?" he said.

She pointed.

"The park, you mean?"

Her voice was soft yet emphatic. "Yes, the park."

He was taken aback. "You talk?"

Turning from him, she opened the door.

"But you're naked!"

She stepped out. Beyond the window, a finger beaconed.

Bob sighed, left the car. He walked with his head down, but a passing mother didn't cover her child's eyes. A policeman on the other side of the road looked his way but kept going.

They reached the entrance. Beyond, the park was small though pleasant, ringed in trees. The woman guided him to a bench by a pond where a paddling of ducks swam. A weeping willow drooped its branches over its left corner; a wooden railing bordered its right. In time, Bob was almost able to forget the city.

"This may sound dumb," he said, "but I've always liked ducks. My mom, she'd take me to the river when I was a kid, and we'd feed them."

There was a tap on his shoulder. He turned, saw the woman's outstretched hand, a slice of bread in her palm.

He didn't question this, just took the offering, tore it into pieces and threw it to the appreciative ducks. "I'm glad you made me come here," he said. "It's good to go out. It's just . . . I'm not a very confident person. Things seem safer when I'm alone." He looked at her. "But maybe that's not—"

He heard something behind him, turned quickly. An elderly couple had entered the park. They appeared content as they walked hand in hand along a circular cobblestone path.

Bob scratched at his neck, debating whether or not he should speak his desire. "Can I hold yours?" he finally asked.

"You may," she said.

His hand trembled but he linked it with hers, watched the ducks and contemplated all the things he'd lost but might regain, turning possibilities over and over in his mind until the sunset colored pond water red and gold.

Night had fallen before Bob

returned home. Though dark, he could see that his box was stuffed with mail, mostly bills. He claimed them before unlocking the door.

Inside, things were in the process of changing again—upholstery looked slick and oily, wallpaper flapped and the TV had grown legs. Bob allowed the woman to enter first.

"Hey," he said. "Fix the TV and maybe we can watch something."

The woman did, but kept going, into the hall.

"Wait. Come back."

Just prior to entering the bedroom, she turned. Again, her finger beaconed.

Bob didn't know what to make of this. He dropped the bills, followed her. Pausing at the door, he saw the woman on the bed, back against the headboard, one leg crooked at the knee. His stomach felt heavy; sweat broke out under his shirt.

"No TV," she said. "Undress."

"But I . . . I—"

She repeated the demand.

He obeyed, but didn't remove his briefs.

"Now come."

Legs wobbled as he made his way to the bed. It was ten feet away, but felt more distant. "Are you sure?" he asked.

She tapped a finger on the mattress.

He sat down on it, covered himself up with sheets quickly, embarrassed that the woman was seeing so much of his body.

She pulled the sheets back down. "Don't," she said.

"But look at me."

"You're fine," she said.

"No, no I'm not."

She stroked his cheek. He pulled away. She leaned over, kissed him on the mouth. He closed it tight. Then a hand was in his underwear. It gripped his cock, squeezing, moving up and down. Forces he thought he'd never feel again started building inside.

"Surrender," she said.

It had been so long since he'd been with a woman, but he couldn't allow himself the pleasure. It was too good for him.

The hand moved faster, tenting blue cotton. "You will surrender."

"But I … I'm a bad man."

"You're not."

He tilted back his head. "God," he said. "You're so beautiful." Then he let his mouth gape.

Slowly, she maneuvered herself atop him.

From the living room, Bob heard the crack of wood and the shriek of metal. It sounded as though the two were grinding against one another, compacting. Never had the things in the house seemed so angry. His penis began to wilt in her grasp.

"Don't listen," she said.

There was noise like clomping feet. Bob turned to the door. Through it, he saw a composite monster. It bounded into the hall, a juggernaut that moved on coat rack legs and flung carpet-roll arms muscled with furniture. The stove was its belly, the fireplace its head.

"Don't look."

"But—"

She pressed her hips into his. "Love me," she said. "Love yourself."

Bob swallowed fear, penetrated her while the monster raised an armchair fist over the bed. The fist slammed into Bob; he felt only pleasure. The monster roared as its component parts loosened, fell to the floor and shattered.

At that very moment, the woman pulled Bob's trigger. He shattered, too. Like bullets, his fragments plowed through and obliterated the things he thought he knew. Time passed without his knowledge until, naked and sweaty, he coalesced in a brighter world. A somehow familiar place, where women were women and guns were guns.

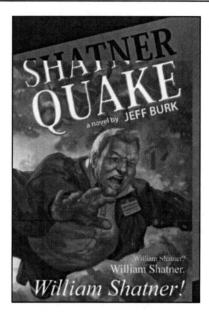

Okay, this is just ridiculous. GOOD! God knows absurdity is its own reward. And even in a voracious consumer culture like ours, there always somehow seems to be more than enough.

But the question is: how much is too much? And the answer is: you're about to find out.

Big thanks and a 20% tip to Mike, who claims "This story was inspired by a seasonal commercial for Red Lobster (which in some cultures, I hear, is a nickname for the Devil)."

Endless Shrimp
by Michael A. Arnzen

It started with the scampi, rammed so tight in the ramekin that I could barely tease the first tail out. The first briny bite was great and garlicky. But little did I realize what I had begun: like tugging some magician's handkerchief, the crustaceans just kept coming: an endless stream of shellfish everywhere I looked. They were festooned on every cocktail the waitress brought. Swimming in every sauce. Piled on every piping hot platter.

It was all I could eat and eventually I cried "no more" and went to pay my bill . . . but the shrimp kept coming: they spilled out of my wallet when I opened it, like a gaggle in a net slopped on deck. When I snatched a fistful of dollar bills, black eyes and red tails squirted between my fingers. Even as I walked to my car, I scratched my ear and a tiny bay shrimp slickered out, pink as a squirming fetus, dropping onto the shoulder of my golden blazer like a dead bird.

I swiped it off and a mass of writhing shrimp poured out from my slimy armpits.

I stared at the growing pile of shrimp at my feet and marveled at the smell before I felt more of the tiny tads—at least nineteen—shooting one bug-eyed bullet after the other—right out of my nose.

The prawns were piling higher and higher around me, and the other people in the parking lot, too, all of us trapped, stunned by the sudden, rising sea of sea creatures, spouting spontaneous from every orifice. I saw cars squishing into the tidal wave of red shrimp spreading down the street as the flood rose up to meet the Red Lobster sign—like the sail of some sinking ship—and many castaways were pulled under the surface around me as I struggled not to drown in their capacious currents.

It was all I could eat.

It was all I could eat.

Robot hillbillies? MY FAVORITE KIND! And count on noted hallucinatory anthropologist Cody Goodfellow to track them in the wild, show them at their noble finest, and thereby enrich our horrible lives.

"Cyberpunk was great when I was growing up," says Cody, "but where were the fucking rednecks? My people had been left behind yet again. In Cyberbilly Heaven, you don't need a catfisting license."

Looping through the curlicues where elaborate genius meets shameless squalor, it's clear that all he really cares about is rupturing your skull. Rest assured he's gonna make you work for the punchline.

I'm betting, once you get there, that you squirt real tears.

Squonk Hunt
by Cody Goodfellow

On a moonless, fog-swaddled Indian summer night, Daddy Huntoon took his best dog and his worst boy into the vast brackish swamp south of Mergatroyd County, hunting for the Squonk.

The sucking black muck rose up to his shoulders, yet Daddy cut through it under full steam without breathing hard, for he sat astride the mighty shoulders of his youngest and dumbest son, Jupiter. Slow but unstoppable, Jupiter trudged across the slimy bottom and paddled with hands like snowshovels, breathing, whenever it occurred to him, through a long, hollow reed.

Daddy Huntoon cut a dashing figure in the misty, mosquito-mad moonlight, with night-vision goggles and a bug-zapper hat perched atop his shrewdly pointed skull. He cradled his blunderbuss up tight under his ingrown chin-whiskers and towed Skillet, a mangy, toothless tick-hound with a jury-rigged two-stroke motor for a brain, by a rusty choke-chain.

When a broad, open channel yawned out of the mangrove trees, Daddy steered Jupiter to shore and alighted on a stump. Skillet limped out of the water and settled down for a nap.

They left the family skimmer in the shallows at the end of the Tarnation County turnpike at sunset, and hoofed it into the deeps. Boats only stirred up trouble at the height of gator mating season, and they hunted skittish prey.

Jupiter loped along in Daddy's wake, a pinheaded avalanche on telephone pole-legs, lugging a harpoon gun and an electrified butterfly net. Every pocket of his overalls was stuffed with loose vittles when they set out, but Jupiter had run through them, and was still hungry enough to eat his own mouth.

Daddy tamped a resinous wad of moonweed into his corncob pipe and crouched to survey the myriad of spoor in the treacherous mud. No man alive could track like Daddy—unless you counted Stookeys, whose kinship with the family of man was a perennial topic of heated local debate—but the uppity swamp kept its own counsel, tonight.

Daddy's hat zapped a wingworm bigger than a fruit bat. Ashes and cremated bits of legs sprinkled into his glowing bowl, but at least the sparking kept Jupiter's attention. Times like this, Daddy could almost picture the critter he suspected was Jupiter's real sire. Whatever it looked like, it was laughing, tonight.

Jupiter's stomach growled fit to fetch a lovestruck she-bear.

"Pussel-gutted bastard!" Daddy cuffed his dearest mistake across the buttocks with the shocky crown of his hat and struck off along the bank.

There had to be an easier way, even out of a boy as dumb and double-ugly as Jupiter, to make a man.

Once a common enough story to find in paper books, folks in Mergatroyd County mislike talk of the Squonk, since the Second War of Northern Aggression brought such dubious wonders to life. Some men stalk it for dreams of wealth and fame, while others have more immediate satisfaction on their minds.

"Wait up, Daddy!" hollered Jupiter. "I's winded!"

"Shut it, Jupe. Tonight, we make a man of you, or eat a bowl of dicks!" Daddy powered up his goggles and swept the tumbling banks of fog, the curtains of moss and vampire vines waving from mangrove trees like castles of melted wax. The branching canals of bubbling murk narrowed and deepened and gnarled into a maze unfit for man or beast. The shore they stood on was a mound of pulverized gator bones, marking the outer boundary of the Stookeys' domain.

Jupiter hustled his nuts and picked his nose with the harpoon. Gibbering a tune about going to meet the finest gal in the hills, he came up short at the verse where he was supposed to describe her. "What she look like, Daddy?"

Daddy puffed his bowl into a white-hot dwarf star. "Nobody knows for certain, boy, but I hear tell she's the most beautiful gal ol' God-daddy ever saw fit to make."

Only smarts the boy ever got were all wasted on his mouth. "If'n nobody know, how you know she pretty? An' if she so pretty, how come she always cry, an' run away?"

Daddy punched Jupiter as high as he could reach, which was yet a mite south of his navel.

"I done tol' you all the tales, sang you all the damned songs, an' you still go on, callin' your Daddy a liar?"

"Daddy, I never said—" Jupiter protested, but dutifully stooped so Daddy could box his ears.

Daddy had, indeed, boned his youngest up on all the lore and hunter's lies about the Squonk, but if you poured a jug of shine into a thimble, most of it was apt to spill.

There was only ever one immortal Squonk, and men spied her only when they got lost in the deep bogs. They heard the creature's pitiable sobbing, but try as they might, even the best trackers seldom bagged her. When they did, the forlorn monster always dissolved in a shower of tears. Some who heard her cry, it was said, fell under the spell of the Squonk, forsaking hearth and home to haunt the swamp, never to return.

Jupiter had showed more sense than was entirely sensible, asking how they could catch the Squonk without melting it, or falling under its spell. Daddy had the stepladder at home, and had administered all kinds of discipline. When he was through, Jupiter asked no more questions. He got born-again committed to the hunt.

As well he should be, since it was on his account, wasn't it? Folks in Mergatroyd had begun to speculate about Jupiter's manhood. Why, even the acephalic warbaby orphan 'Bama, who was nothing but thin air above his goonish smile, had sired three litters of babies among the trashier clans in Trailertown, and God only knew how many more, among the hapless animal kingdom.

Doc Caulweather, Widow Cooney and the veterinary mech had all examined him, and judged Jupiter's tackle was adequate to the task; but to Daddy Huntoon's undying shame, Jupiter proved too dense an idiot manchild to hear Nature's call, so it had come to this.

Daddy wanted more for his youngest son than just a roll with a boxhead whore at the roadhouse, the Cockatrices the Stookeys ran with in the Hollows, or arranged marriage to a dumpy Dry County sow, like his Daddy did for him. Although the best part of Jupiter was, sad to say, a heart-shaped stain on the seat of the truck in which he was conceived and birthed, he was still a Huntoon.

Daddy flipped a switch on his big silver belt buckle. Skillet twitched and jolted on invisible strings until he locked on a scent, then galloped off, baying at the moon, to the limit of his chain. Sparks and curls of blue smoke popped from his brainbox.

"Ol' Skillet's got the scent," crowed Daddy. "Don't you, boy? Her witchy-mone trail goes through there like a skunk sign, boy. We ain't far off."

It took Jupiter a spell to decipher, but finally, he clapped his hubcap hands and did a jig. "You smart, Daddy."

Like fire eating a trail of gunpowder, Skillet ran down the perverse spoor of the Squonk, spooking goony birds and bog-trotting octopi with his fretful bark. Deeper they plunged into the swamp, slogging and battling through orgies of amorous gators; skirting stagnant, bottomless pools hiding giant snapping turtles with whole human skulls in their shit; skulking, with ears and noses stopped up tight against witchery, past the stilt-walking shack of the Mergatroyd Hag.

Soon enough, they were truly and totally lost. Daddy waded up onto a sandbar to take account of the stars when he blundered into a lively mess of crafty black tentacles. They whipped him up like a hare in a rope snare, then sucked him under so fast Jupiter saw only the splash, and Daddy's bug-zapper hat spinning in the air.

Strings of bubbles stuffed with cussing breached the pudding-skin surface, but presently, the bog burst asunder from Daddy firing his blunderbuss deep down in the slime.

Petrified between dueling Gorgons of fear—the unknown and Daddy—Jupiter could only gawk, bellowing, "Where Daddy?" and eating the mosquitoes that alit in his gaping mouth. It fell to Skillet to tow Daddy to safety.

No sooner was Daddy shut of the last flechette-peppered tentacle, when Jupiter trampled him, running in panicked circles on a taut, sticky tether, flattening Daddy twice more before Daddy puzzled it out.

One of Jupiter's huge, hammy arms was wrapped up in the tongue of a granddaddy hellbender. He chased himself round the misbegotten giant newt, just like Skillet did, whenever his battery backup died.

Daddy took up Jupiter's harpoon gun. He had to brace it on his knee, and could barely cock it, but he neatly skewered the hellbender's huge froggy head through the roof of its mouth, pinning it to a fallen log. Monster's tongue was so tough that Daddy polished off a pouch of shine and Skillet took a nap before Jupiter gnawed the stubborn appendage off at the root and dragged it along behind.

And deeper still . . .

Skillet lost the scent in a channel of putrid ooze dammed up with charred Chinese space station junk. Daddy crossed it piggyback atop Jupiter, with Skillet paddling frantically in front, his brainbox chugging like a weed-whacker cutting kudzu.

"Daddy, we there yet?" Jupiter piped, whenever he came up for air.

Daddy steered the ungrateful lummox onto an oil drum beach. Jupiter discovered the severed hellbender tongue still stuck to his arm, and happily chewed on it.

Skillet growled and pointed like a hood ornament on a banker's fancy car.

Daddy hushed him and slipped on his goggles. The musky witchy-mones of their quarry hung so thick on the air that even Daddy could feel it, and not just with his upstairs senses.

The goggles outlined the night in bold, sun-bright lines against sweaty green shadows. Over the next rise and through a patch of nightlight fungi, the all-powerful aroma reeled them in like catfish too dumb to fight. The indigo glow of the mushrooms bedeviled his goggles, but he still picked out fading heat-spoor meandering off into a lonesome lagoon. A dappling of caustic will-o-wisp lights danced over the three-toed footprints written on the water.

Zeroed in on the trail, Daddy saw each print glow hotter than the last, hotter still, hottest . . .

"Judas git home," Daddy whispered, "there she is."

For just a second, no hunger or lust could shake Daddy's wonder at the sight and scent of the curvy, girl-shaped slice of sunfire perched atop the vine-wreathed fuselage of an old-time chopper gunship. And the sound she made . . .

Skillet stood up on arthritic hind legs and danced with blood-frenzy. Daddy misliked the thought of the scrambled hound eating Jupiter's intended. He went for the POWER switch on his belt marked DOG. Beside it, he had a switch for TRUCK, and another for WIFE, but they were long since broken.

Skillet's brainbox shut off with a sputter and more smoke, and the old hound collapsed like a string-cut puppet. Nothing stood between the Huntoons and the mournful sobbing song of the Squonk.

Jupiter rocked beside him to the bodice-ripping harmony, monsoon raindrops of drool pattering on his belly, but the miscegenated idiot was no more nor less poleaxed then his Daddy.

All Daddy had to say was, "Now," and Jupiter would pounce. Boy couldn't eat without biting his own fingers, but he could run for days, and if you told him to catch the sun, he'd chase it to China. But all of a sudden, "Now" was a very long word, a boring speech in a foreign tongue.

The cries of the Squonk bewitched the whole danged swamp to lie still. It was almost a song, like a mockingbird or a jinglebug—pattern enough to beguile you into pity, chaos enough to nail you to lust. Subhuman, yet it overflowed with superhuman grief. No human or mankin could bear an hour under such a punishing sadness; they would kill themselves or keel over with their hearts cracked in twain. The Squonk wept for its ugliness, and it seemed a cruel trick for God-daddy to put such powerful sense into such a godawful face. Daddy kept the goggles' resolution just low enough to see her fine enough outline.

The Squonk was a critter, but also, undeniably, a woman. Daddy well knew how women saw only flaws in the mirror, just as he knew how to comfort them in those short, sweet days when they were wrong.

Strange, but it didn't raise Daddy's hackles the way women's weeping always did. He had no urge to slap it; the urge he did feel cut against his grain, but he dreamed of taking it in his arms, not as a hunted beast, but as a man takes a woman—

"God's balls, it's witchcraft!" Daddy primed the launcher under the barrel of his blunderbuss and discharged a milky white torrent that turned solid in midair and clothed the shamelessly cavorting critter in a rubbery net. "I got her, boy! I got—"

The Squonk bolted. Even mummied up in the silicon webbing, she dragged Daddy Huntoon like a monster truck through the muddy lagoon and off into the trees.

Jupiter doggedly plodded after them with his charged butterfly net. About a mile deeper into the swamp, he caught up close enough to snare Daddy's head, and shocked him stupid.

Try as he might to dig in his heels, Jupiter slid, slipped, fell on his face and got dragged. The Huntoons together weighed less than an empty promise, for all they slowed the galloping Squonk.

And then, Jupiter hit a stump. It missed both his legs, but stopped him dead, and made him scream louder and higher and sadder than the sorrowful beast they'd caught. Anchored by Jupiter's considerable groin, the chase finally ground to a halt.

Daddy woke up in quicksand up to his belly, but he still clung to the gun like grim death. At the end of its tether, the Squonk wailed like a white lightning hangover. Its struggles were at an end. It almost broke him, to hear that pitiful note of surrender, but Daddy was no mere man. He was a Huntoon.

Daddy dragged the thrashing bundle close and bashed it over the head with his blunderbuss. At last, it fell silent.

Jupiter loped up, rubbing mud into his crotch. "Now what, Daddy?"

Daddy stood with one bootless foot on the flank of his catch. "Jupiter Huntoon, this is your day. Now, it ain't the normal way, but as no woman in Mergatroyd County, in or out of the clan, will have you, it falls to you to tame the wild Squonk, and so become a man. Are you ready, boy?"

Jupiter swatted at the flies that always came buzzing round his head when he tried to think.

Daddy stroked his boy's back like burping a baby. "Now, what you see with the Squonk ain't exactly what you get, y'hear? It'll bewitch you into thinkin' she's powerful ugly, but at the same time . . ."

Jupiter picked his nose and ate the leech he found amongst his boogers. "Aw, Daddy, I don't want no ugly gal . . . an' what about the curse?"

With the deed so close to done, Daddy tried manfully to be soothing, so as not to spook the boy. "That's old maid talk, son. Women spread that story to stop menfolk chasing the Squonk, but men of the world, like us, we know the truth . . ."

"What's that, Daddy?"

"The magic is in them tears. Those tears have a powerful charm, which makes men mad with lust, and ignites fires in the blood. Only a real man can survive its burnination, but then no woman can resist *him*, see?"

"Why it always crying, Daddy?"

Daddy sheared the silicon net away with a wicked bowie knife, and laid the creature bare. "How the hell should I know? Now get your damned drawers off, before the damned critter melts . . ."

Jupiter didn't obey, but Daddy didn't hit him.

The Squonk—she—lay naked and helpless between them. A vile hybrid of opossum and amphibian, yet the Squonk was no more nor less than a hot eight-breasted chick from the neck down, albeit with loose, warty skin that slid lasciviously across its inviting chassis like a wet silk nightgown. Its great, veiny bat ears, feathery tufted gills, lidless bubble-eyes and tendril-festooned snout only riled Daddy all the more for their unholy fusion to such voluptuous beauty.

The trembling Squonk cringed with its forepaws over its gruesome face and wept sweet streams of black molasses tears. Daddy averted his eyes and tried to remember a prayer. Jupiter was lost in contemplation.

"No man who ever returned has been strong enough to withstand the lovin' of the Squonk, boy! If you do this, you'll bask in the awe of kin and strangers alike. Nobody'll ever dare to call you stupid or beat on you ever again, son. You'll be a man! An' if it goes ill for you, I ain't got no shortage of sons . . ."

Jupiter yawned. "I dunno, Daddy . . ."

Daddy tuned him up with the blunderbuss, but he had no heart for it. "You dadgum idiot! Got to strike fast, or she'll melt in her own tears! Boy, I'll . . . just have to . . . show you . . . how it's done . . . Oh, my Gawd . . ."

Daddy looked again at the Squonk, and beheld the creature transformed wholly into a beautiful woman, a weeping preacher's daughter crouching in the slime with her backside fetched up high to beckon him closer.

"You . . . harlot . . . Jezebel . . . get thee behind me . . ."

Daddy rebuked her, and yet his bib overalls slipped off as he fell upon her. Parting the satiny pantaloon folds of her hind legs, he mounted her from behind and plowed the lagoon with the wailing face of the writhing Squonk.

"Oh, you Whore of Babylon," he roared in glossolalian ecstasy, "you black she-goat, abgablabluhkabab, shabashothoogablahhh!"

The bodacious swamp critter wriggled like a ferret in rut, twisting double on itself and climbing the air, clawing his thighs bloody while humping Daddy as no earthly woman could be paid or charmed to do.

How long it went on, only Jupiter could tell, and he never learned to read a digital watch. At last, Daddy let fly a rebel yell from the soles of his feet, and spent his seed.

In Daddy's moment of greatest weakness, the wily critter toppled him and drove him under the black water.

The bubbles came few and far between to the surface, but Daddy put up no fight as the Squonk tried to drown him with her tears.

"Hey!" Jupiter sprang into alertness. "Where Daddy?"

The Squonk knelt over Daddy, wracked by fatal waves of sobbing. Jupiter smacked her, and slashed her head clean off.

Crying out in horror, he tried to make it right. But it was too late. All at once, the Squonk dissolved into whittled water, and was no more.

Jupiter fished for Daddy. "Daddy? What you do to her? Where my gal go?"

Daddy Huntoon rose up out of the swamp, mud streaming off his shorted-out hat, the brim drooping down over his face. "HOOOOOWEEE!!! Boy, that was sweet . . . Hey, where'd she go? Damn, boy, did you let

her get loose?"

The idiot manchild's wounded stare and the salty taste on his tingling lips told Daddy what happened. "You stupid bastard, I tol' you to hurry! You cain't be no fruit of my loins, 'cos now you ain't never gonna be a man!"

Jupiter looked confused, but then his thick lips squirmed into a gobsmacked grin. "There you are . . ."

Skillet growled and whined, just behind him. Belt must've shorted out, too. Skillet was a damn good dog. The old hunting hound still had the scent. Green sparks spat from his brainbox.

"What the hell're you smilin' at, Jupe?"

Daddy Huntoon reached out to box Jupiter's ears but good, when he took note of the daintily webbed forepaw with which he did it.

He ogled his reflection in the water and let out a mournful wail that still bewitched him, even now that it came from his own throat.

Daddy's wiry old body had softened and filled out like a thirsty sponge, soaking up the sizzling gumbo of swampwater and Squonk tears. Bones turned to rubber and warped him onto all fours. Lean coils of swamp-rat muscle and lush mounds of sleek feminine flesh swelled under the loose, warty velveteen folds of his skin.

Worst of all, his proud Huntoon face, chiseled by generations of selective inbreeding, rotted off while something wet and raw and red pushed out through it. Seeing that tendril-whiskered possum-frog mask in the black liquid mirror, what else could he do, but howl?

Jupiter was slow as a cement enema, but he could sometimes learn to do a job, if you showed him how. His empty eyes glazed over and his tongue hung down to his Adam's apple, ripping his overalls off as he ogled the newborn Squonk.

"Daddy . . . you . . . purty!"

And Daddy learned, at last, why the Squonk cries.

Most Bizarro stories don't demand that you race toward the dictionary, just to figure out if the title is actually a word. That's more of a highbrow science fiction trick.

But in this case, I urge you to look it up, once you're done puzzling out the rest of the freakishness on display in Livia's unsettling voyeuristic fucktasmagoria.

"From the windows of my tenement apartment," she says, "I can see into the windows of four giant factory/warehouse buildings, all of which have been converted into luxury condos. It can be quite a show at night, but like the protagonist in my story, I always want to see more . . ."

Panopticon
by Livia Llewellyn

Is this you?

There is a place deep in the warehouse district, far outside the civilized edges of the city called Obsidia, where the population bleeds off into cul-de-sacs and dead-end roads, where only abandoned brick buildings and crumbling smokestacks remain. You have heard of this place solely by learning to phrase the questions as though they were snowflakes falling from the sky—questions outside your control, beyond your care or concern. Questions like that are answered in the passage of time, eventually: by cracked nails pressed against yellowing maps of long-dead subway lines, words parsed from veins of blood welling from a blossoming wound, grunts behind locked bathroom doors that echo out numbers, names. Answers, in the smoky plume of the dragon, the sour tang of the drug. And over the years and decades, you bead the collected answers onto the needle-fine wire of your need: gradually a map appears, a date, a time. You will not hold this information a second time: the invitation, like a comet, will pass from your view into the black of night, never to be seen in your lifetime again.

It never occurs to you not to go. In a way, you're already there.

Is this you?

Wheels screech against tracks, and sparks bounce off the pitted concrete walls. The train shudders as it plunges underground, and your cotton skirt slides with you over the curve of the orange plastic seat. No one else is in the car, so you slip onto the raised bump between seats, letting the V of the ridge rest firm between your legs. It calms you. Spaces are meant to be filled.

Opposite, posters fill the space between the windows and doors. Women and men with once-glowing cheeks and plump lips hold bottles of effervescing liquids, or lounge on sleek leather Biedermeiers, gazing through curtainless windows into Obsidia's glorious silver horizon, into a future that will never be. Their faces are faded, melted and mottled from mold, humidity, and relentless plumes of metallic smoke. The engines shudder again, and fluorescent panels buzz and wink out, one by one. At each far end, windows glow, illuminating the cars before and behind. You stand up and walk forward, your hand gripping the filthy poles and bars to keep your balance. The door to the next carriage is locked: you peer through the grimy windows and across a small rattling platform into sulphur-tinged light, your breath fogging the glass.

They can't see you, the couple in the car. You stand in black, swaying in time with the pitch of the train, watching the woman's head jerk back and forth. A man stands before her, hands clasping the looped bars overhead. His pants hang below the curve of his naked ass, and he thrusts his pelvis forward and back, in time to the rocking of the car. You move to the window's side, and catch flashes of long, wet cock, thrusting to and fro in the woman's mouth and hands. The flesh between your legs swells and thickens in the heat, and your fingers twitch: but you turn away, walk back into the empty dark of the car, whispering a number, a name. The train seem to sigh in return, murmuring hot phrases of love. So easy, to lean against the trembling doors. The upturned handles, so very hard, so warm . . .

Not yet, you whisper in the dark to the racing machines, to your racing heart.

Not yet.

Is this you?

The afternoon is the caramel shade of fossilized saurian bone, hardened and inured to the passage of time. You walk down streets razed by wind and dust into thin crusts of cobblestone and tar, the destination always on the tip of your tongue like the taste of anthracite coal. Signs have long decayed into dust in this part of the city, and only ravens and dogs know the lay of the land. But the jewels of information gathered over the years are a crown, and for this single day you are Queen. And the kingdom waits. Left of the summit breaker, her broken windows winking like sequins on a dead bride's gown. Right of the seven brick stacks, blackened with centuries and cloaked in webs of dead vines. Across the iron bridge and over the Mannequin Sea, its million sloe-eyed beauties jumbled below like broken teeth against a giant's fist. Painted, flaking pupils stare up at you, a stagnant sea of watchers: you look away, and run. Through the endless warehouse rows, low grey bunkers like scabs on necrotized flesh, long emptied of goods and dreams. You squat once, by the side of the road, and watch the strand of urine slither into the street, seep into the cracks of the worn stones. In seconds, all traces of you disappear. For one fearful moment, you see yourself as though through distant glass: cunt pressed onto the smooth rock, cobblestones melting and pressing up through the wet folds, the stony cock of the world fucking and drilling into your soul. You rise, scurry away. The cracked stones beneath your feet shift and moan.

At the end of the warehouses, a single building stands, framed by two coke quenching towers. A blast furnace winds its way into the center of the brick, pipes as wide as buildings split into massive V's that cast shadows into the sunless sky. Beyond the building, Obsidia disappears, as if the earth itself ends. This is it. There is nothing beyond.

Cracked engines line the walkway leading up broken steps to a single open door, leading into a void. You check your watch. You know the time to enter. You sit on an engine, in the shadow of the furnace, and wait.

Is this you?

At the right hour, at the right minute, when the seconds have burned away like beads of sweat on a lover's shivering back, you rise and walk with stiff legs up the steps. The air is still and thick, with motes of dust hanging about you like drifting spiders. The light ends in a clean line as you pass through the door, into a hallway that pierces through the wide factory space. If anyone else is here, you cannot hear them, cannot smell them. The dirt beneath your feet lays undisturbed. Those who dwell here did not come this way. Behind you, the door closes, the day disappears. Somewhere in the building, machines spring into life, their rhythmic thunder reverberating through the walls.

Doors line the hall, but you do not touch the knobs as you pass by, though they look warm and inviting. None of those doors lead to what you were instructed to seek, what you asked to see. You walk carefully, one hand raised to brush stray webs from your face: as an afterthought, you look up. If there is a ceiling, it is not visible to your small human eyes. The walls rise straight up, as if into stars. You feel naked, as if something has peeled the edges of space away, inserting its gaze through dark matter and time all the way into the sticky center of your bones.

In the gloom, a pale sulphur glow of light flares into life: a beacon, beckoning. You approach, your fingers brushing over the mound beneath your skirt. The glass is curved at the edges, like the windows of the subway car, and rimmed by strips of hard rubber. Like aquarium glass: thick enough to keep the two worlds, the wet and the dry, from commingling. Palms flat against the glass, you lean forward, until the tip of your nose hits the surface, and your breath flows from your lips back into your mouth. Your body settles against the door—not a door, really, but an end, a terminus—and finds the ridged curves of a handle, smooth and warm, perfectly positioned by your accommodating, hidden hosts. Vibrations from the unseen machines whoosh throughout the building like blood through veins, into the quivering brass. The fabric of your skirt grows damp. The light in the other room intensifies. And now you see.

Is this you?

In the next room, a crowd of people clump together in the confined tube of a shuddering subway car, their faces blank, like melting ice. A woman sits on the plastic bench, one leg hitched up and resting on the orange curves of the preformed seat to her side. Her dark hair floats like a mourning veil in wind, obscuring her face. On the floor before her, a man crouches, his tongue and lips moving over the red folds of her cunt, barely visible through the long, unruly V of black hair that envelopes it. The metal and glass before you is as impenetrable as a blast door, yet you swear you can hear the sound of her breath bleeding into your ears, hear the subtle wet sounds of the man's tongue lapping, drawing the liquid out of her. The brass handle shudders and slips against your raw skin: your skirt is bunched around your waist, but you don't remember raising it. You push your groin forward, gasping as the woman thrusts against the man, straining her body against his large hands. Claw-like nails bite into her thighs, and where they strafe her skin, rubies ooze from the flesh, clattering onto the floor. The standing, swaying men and women ignore them: they have no ears, no eyes, no mouths. Only you see the man's hideous, lupine face, his darting tongue; only you smell the sea salt folds of the woman's flesh; only you hear the leviathan sounds well from her throat as she comes, the noise as deep and dark as the engines below. Only you asked to see.

The man rises, almost unfolding his bulky mass into the small space, pushing against the other commuters to make room. They clatter against each other, and you start in shock as a pale arm drops from a sleeve and floats to the ceiling. Another arm drops, followed by a head. One by one, the people crumble into brittle, bloodless pieces. Were they ever alive? Snowflakes of flesh and bone drift and knock about in the hot, noisy air. The car flooded and they are underwater, you realize, and the crowd nothing more than mannequins. But, then, how do the man and woman breathe?

The man brushes the bodies away like fire pushing through grass. He is all impassive muscles and phallus, every part of him forged. Diamonds and pearls ooze from the tip of his purple cock in liquid strands, spilling down the woman's breasts. She reaches up to brush them away, but the man grabs her thighs and lifts her torso high into the air, impaling her onto his cock as easily as if she were a summer cotton dress, to be bent and torn at will. Between your legs, the metal shifts and pierces upward, as if into your heart: the pain is so great, you cannot speak. Your nails claw at the glass, and small squeaks fill the burning air. Within the car, the woman slides onto the man, and sapphires bleed from her eyes; she opens her mouth, and more rubies stream out, emeralds and opals and stars. The man is a piercing sword, a burning blade, a broken train, and finally, finally, her head whips back and all that black hair floats away as she sees you, you see you and you see her and you both scream don't, stop, don't stop. Not yet.

You want to see it all.

Before you, the woman splits apart. Her limbs join the others, drifting in the ruby sea. They were not mannequins, after all. The man pushes her torso off his cock, thick pearls of semen dribbling in strands from the purple tip. They brush across your face, droplets catching in the curves of your mouth. The taste is flame and oil, and you feel your skin peel away. You never left the subway train. You never wandered an abandoned kingdom of wonders, you never entered a hall of a million doors. You never received answers to all the questions you asked. You do not watch. You were never the audience. You were the space, the void. In the distance, sighs and faint applause; and the unseen engine winds down, each thunderous pound like a bead falling off a strand, with more and more space in between. Until, there is no sound at all, not even the crackle of fire or drip of blood. There is only you as the metal thrusts up past the walls of your cunt and splits you apart, you looking up past the endless walls past the brief flash pleasure into all-consuming frenzy of pain, you floating through a ruby ocean of your own making into a space where all the stars look down on you, and all the stars are eyes.

And yet. And yet.
You still see.
Were you wrong? Is there more?
Is this really you?

Overhead, the slender pedestrian bridge stands fast against a saurian colored sky. Your painted, flaking pupils see it in slices, only through the rigid fingers of a hand—whose hand it is, you cannot tell. There are hands all around you, feet and torsos and heads, but you do not feel them as much as sense that they are there, jumbled about like autumn leaves. Like snow. You cannot feel any part of your body, or if it even remains a part of you. Maybe in some near acre or field, your hand obscures the view of other eyes, another face. Occasional storms smear black clouds overhead, and sometimes night falls, though it does not fall often in this forgotten district of Obsidia. Yet, the view never changes. Always and only, you see the bridge, the fingers, the bird-free sky.

Although, once in a very long while, you spy movement on the bridge, the hesitant gait of a traveler, a seeker crossing the iron trestles. They are heading toward a place they've only heard of in half-spoken words, coils of smoke and spatterings of blood. You see the traveler, fix your unmoving eye upon their familiar, yearning face, and the slender line of metal will become a hallway, a black vein that bleeds out into a trillion desires, then endless horror, then beyond. You want to cry out, *I know this woman, I know this journey, this place. Turn back. Don't go.* But your fading lips cannot part, and your torso is a hollow void. All you can do is watch with lidless eyes, watch each traveler arrive at the destination of their own making, and wait for the day when the sun runs down and the stars burn out in the sky, when there is nothing more to see, because there is nothing more. And then you will have what you asked for, so very long ago.

You will have seen it all.
This is you.

This is that rare piece of truly emotional Bizarro, and the only story herein that makes me cry every time I read it. It's something I'd like to see happen more often.

Simply told and deeply felt and dripping with benevolent strangeness, I love this one with all my heart.

Marcy wishes to say, "Dance at My Funeral is dedicated to Hollis Charles (February 22, 1939 - March 26, 2003). I was lucky enough to have known a man who lived with joy in his pocket."

Dance at My Funeral
by Marcy Italiano

"I can't do this." Cara twisted a strand of her long brown hair into a knot.

"You can. For Robert, you can." John rolled up the car window as they pulled into the parking lot. "I've been to a couple of funerals before; I'll help you through this."

"You're right. I'll do my best . . . Am I going to have to see his body?"

"Probably. Yes."

Cara took a deep breath as John pulled into a parking spot. All she knew was that she had to wear black, and that she would have to meet his family and say . . . something.

It seemed impossible that Robert could die.

Cara remembered the day she started smoking. A little bell rang when she stepped into the store, and a black man smiled at her. Not knowing what to choose from behind the counter, she tried to sound confident and asked for what he thought was the best brand.

His Jamaican accent was thick, "It depends on what's been troublin' ya, hun. I need to know more about ya. This is a serious decision, one that sticks with ya for life, brands such as these. Do you have some time for a conversation?"

Fuck. He wasn't going to sell to her. "Uh, not today. Not that you'd want to hear about my shit anyway. I'll just buy some gum." Her hand still shook as she handed him the money. She just wanted to get out of there.

"Well, when you come back, I'll be here again, and I'll have more gum for ya, hun!" It almost sounded like he said rum. She smiled on her way out the door.

When she stepped out onto the sidewalk, a few of her friends laughed, and one gave her a smoke instead. She could feel the Jamaican man inside watching over her while she choked and struggled to inhale as her friends coached her.

The following week, Cara walked into the store and asked for a pack of king size Rothman's. She had the money out of her pocket already, but her hand still shook when she placed it on the counter.

"But I still don't know anything about ya. That may not be the right one for ya. Listen, my name is Robert. I have a chair that's always here by the counter, and I neeever go anywhere." He laughed so loud it filled the whole store and melted her smoke-denial frustration.

She introduced herself and said, "So, you just let people hang around here then? Like, just to fuck around? Aren't you afraid of people stealing shit?"

"If you're talking to me, then I've got my eye on ya, don't I?" He winked at her.

She eyed the empty chair. "Maybe I'll stop by sometime. We'll see. Y'know, like, if I don't have better shit to do first."

"I'd be honoured to be better than your shit, hun." Cara laughed with him as she left the store.

Cara knew that she had met someone special, regardless of the strange circumstances. On Friday afternoons, she went to the store, and was always greeted with a boisterous, exaggerated accent, "Cara! Daalin', how aaa you!" They talked for hours as customers came and left. She'd duck out for smoke breaks and eat the pre-wrapped subs. He listened, they laughed, she cried when she told him about what was really going on in her life. When a customer commented on their conversation, she told them to fuck off. Robert told Cara that even though most people are so very stupid, she needed to listen for when the few smart ones came along. He was the craziest sane person she knew.

But he wasn't supposed to die. Cara didn't even know how he died, he'd just disappeared one day and a new lady told her where she could find him.

She got out of John's car and tried to walk gracefully across the parking lot in high heels. She planned to sneak into the crowd at the funeral to pay her respects, say her own little goodbye to Robert, and leave as quickly as possible.

When they walked around the building to the front doors, they saw a large crowd of people on the sidewalk. As they got closer, they saw that a number of people looked strangely excited, and they could hear pieces of odd-sounding conversation.

John bumped into a black man with a moustache and heard him say, "The Shaman has come!"

Cara excused herself to walk in front of a Chinese lady who said, "I can't wait to see it!"

They overheard an Irish woman saying, "Such an honour . . ."

Cara and John were puzzled. There were people of all races and backgrounds talking in a buzz, flooding the cement walkway. Robert was a wonderful man and obviously had many friends, but she couldn't make sense of such excitement at a funeral. Cara's frown grew deeper. She squeezed her hands into fists and bit her lip as they proceeded to the front doors.

Once inside, the funeral director asked if they had come to see Robert one last time. Cara nodded.

"Are you related, or a friend of the family?"

"A friend." Cara whispered.

"Please find your way to the Hallman Room, the large one down the hall, on your left." The Funeral Director pointed.

Creamy walls, deep green carpets, and lush, burgundy furniture almost went unnoticed behind the crowd. In the middle of the hallway there was a clearing around someone sitting down. People were pointing and staring at an older man seated in a little wooden chair off to the side.

She heard again and again, "Shaman . . ."

Having grown up Catholic and not knowing much about other beliefs, Cara assumed he was a type of priest from another religion. She and John continued walking to the Hallman Room. She tried to figure out what she was going to say to Robert's family members. She'd practiced a sombre "I'm sorry" and wished she could say something more respectable, more *personal*, without sounding like some crazy nut off the street. She doubted they could ever understand her very short but very intense connection with Robert.

Cara prepared herself to see an open coffin. It was not going to be her friend. It was just a dead body. A corpse. Fear struck her; the reality of death stopped her breath in her throat. She tried to hold on to the memories of the person she knew before looking at his motionless face. She took a deep breath and walked in.

Robert's family stood along the front and sides of the room, one by one shaking hands, hugging, and occasionally leaving lipstick on someone's cheek. Some were gently smiling. Others had watery eyes and a shaky lip. Some were at peace already. Or maybe in shock. It was hard to tell.

Moving further into the room and looking between family members, Cara could see parts of a glass box instead of a wooden coffin. She felt herself starting to panic.

It's not just an open coffin, I can see right through the whole thing!

She'd never heard of anything like this before. She tried to make herself approach the box. She forced images into her mind from the last time she and Robert sat in the store, chatting about a fight she'd had with a friend. How trivial. She could feel John's hand on her shoulder, which helped her move forward.

She kept her gaze down, watching her shoes move along the carpet until they met up with the glass case stand. Before she looked up John whispered, "Dear God."

Cara didn't know how Robert died. Hearing John's reaction did not make her want to look. She shut her eyes as hard as she could. She didn't have to look, did she? Nobody would be able to tell. Her back was facing the rest of the room. She heard John stutter.

"I . . . I . . . that's . . . why the . . . what the. . ."

He was scaring her. She had to look. After all, if it was an open casket of sorts, this glass case. Robert couldn't be in that bad of shape.

She opened her eyes slowly, trying to take in one part of the body at a time.

First she saw the fingertips of Robert's right hand and then the cuff of his suit jacket. Nice cufflinks. She continued to look up his arm. She was breathing heavily. Something was wrong.

Cara looked carefully at Robert's elbow. His arm had been . . . *separated*, cut off at the elbow. But it wasn't just lying there as if it had been severed in an accident. Where the elbow should have been there were neatly rounded wooden stubs with a metal hook and eye joining them together. It made his arm look like a prosthetic puppet limb.

Trying to comprehend what she was seeing, Cara raised her gaze a little higher along the body. She held her hand over her mouth, trying not to make a sound. At the top of his arm, again, were wooden stumps instead of a shoulder joint, with a silver hook on his arm and a loop on his torso.

She put her hands gently on John's arm to hold herself up. Both of Robert's arms were taken apart in the same manner. His legs were also severed into pieces at the knees and hips with larger, shiny hooks and loops. Each piece of his body lay on a satin pillow.

Everyone else in the room seemed to be fine with this. Nobody was bothered by the mutilation. Some looked almost *giddy*. Did they even know what horrible atrocity had happened at the front of the room? Did they see what had been done to Robert's body?

"He's coming! Everybody, stand back, please," a stranger's voice called out.

Cara forced herself to take one last look at Robert's face. She nearly passed out, and John had to catch her with the little strength *he* had left before they moved back with the crowd.

Robert's head had been hollowed out. Only the front half of his skull with his face was left. It still looked like his living face, just in the form of a mask. Cara whimpered. She tried to figure out why anyone would do such a thing, and why nobody seemed alarmed!

Moving off to the side, Cara and John nearly bumped into a set of steel drums. A woman close by noticed Cara's panicked state and quickly whispered in her ear, "Did nobody tell you?"

The old man who had been sitting on the little chair walked slowly through the center of the room. He looked frail and shortened by his old age.

"It is time. Everyone we need is here." He stopped for a moment to look at each person in the room, including Cara and John. "I knew you would all come. Robert was a very good, dear of mine. It is my pleasure and great honour to be able to do this for him, and for all of his friends and family. Please know that I will take good care of Robert. I'll make sure he gets to where he is going. But first, we will become one, and we will dance, and you will dance with us until we are tired. Then we will all sleep peacefully." He smiled.

The old man turned around and opened the top of the glass case. With help from some men that Cara thought were pallbearers, they lifted Robert's torso out of the case, and held it face out to the rest of the room.

The old man stepped up behind the body, putting his face into Robert's hollowed-out head as the others strapped the torso to his body. Cara could see the old man's eyes through Robert's empty sockets.

Someone must have put a chair behind her for her safety, because she didn't remember intentionally sitting down. Surely she was having a nightmare.

One piece at a time, first the upper arms and then the lower arms, the men caringly hooked Robert's limbs to the torso. The old man held the hands by the wrists. Next they hooked on Robert's thighs, and then strapped on his lower legs and feet.

The old man made a muffled joke through the Robert-mask, "It seems I'm not as tall as I used to be; his feet are going to have to stand on mine with his knees bent. I'm going to teach Robert how to dance the same way we teach all of our children!"

The crowd chuckled. They tied Robert's shoes to the tops of the old man's bare feet. The woman who whispered to her before leaned over again and said, "Just try and enjoy it. You'll be glad you did when it's all over."

Cara looked at her, blinked, and couldn't speak.

Once the old man was hooked onto Robert completely the steel drums started.

The music rang out, and the old man wiggled his butt, using Robert like a marionette. He shook and waved Robert's hands, shuffled Robert's feet to the music. A Caribbean beat filled the room, bounced off of the walls. The drums chimed back and forth in harmony.

The old man shouted out and motioned for people to join him.

Slowly, family members and friends bobbed their heads, moved their hips, and tapped their feet. Most people didn't start to dance until the Shaman invited them one by one.

As the drums beat out a cheerful tune, men and women joined the old man, even holding Robert's hands while dancing. Some of the ladies kissed Robert's face. They were laughing with him, hugging him and yelling out, "You're wonderful, baby!"

Cara forced back bile as she watched in horror. John squatted beside her, also unable to stand. She wanted to run, to get out of this place. She didn't. She didn't want anyone to notice her. She wanted to just disappear into the walls. She wanted to pretend that this day

505

never happened, that she wasn't really seeing the disgusting performance before her.

As she looked around for a plant to throw up in discreetly, she didn't notice the old man walking straight towards them.

"Cara! Daalin', how aaa you!" It was Robert's voice. It was the same way he greeted her every time she went to visit him.

Cara looked up from her carpet-trance, stunned. What had looked like a mask was now Robert's whole face again. The hooks were gone, arms and legs complete, the puppetry no longer apparent.

She forgot about the old man, and she forgot that Robert had died. She looked into his eyes—*his* eyes—and was completely swept away.

"Come, Cara! Come and dance with me!" He smiled from ear to ear as he laughed, and did a little toe-tappin' dance move that made her giggle.

It was wonderful to hear his laugh again. Her heart instantly lightened, even as her eyes overflowed, remembering the first time Robert made her laugh until she cried.

Cara tried not to stumble in her heels on the carpet. Robert told her she looked like a princess and moved like a ballerina, and it made her laugh through her tears. Cara held out her hands and allowed Robert to lead her around the room once more. The rest of the family clapped along and smiled at them. It felt so good, so relaxed and natural, to be in his company.

When he let go of Cara's hand, he reached out for John's. Robert made sure each person felt a part of the revelry.

The crowd danced for hours. Nobody stopped moving. The drums kept chiming. The sun went down, and the lights in the room seemed to flicker between the dancing bodies.

But they could only dance for so long.

Robert walked over to the people playing the steel drums; and as he thanked them one by one, they put down their mallets and stood still.

The room calmed down, the laughter subdued, and the dancing stopped. Everyone applauded and cheered. Robert made everyone feel exhilarated.

Cara clapped and then started to cry. This was the end.

"Thank you, everyone! I love you all very, OH so very much! Thank you for coming to dance at my funeral. But I am very tired now, and I have to go to sleep." He held out his arms, then clasped his hands together one last time and held them in front of his body as he walked through the center of the room.

As he passed each person, they quietly said, "Goodbye, Robert."

Robert looked straight ahead, smiled, but was careful not to look anyone in the eyes. He wanted to leave this world remembering only the dancing, not the tears.

He walked closer to Cara. It was the last time she would speak to him. It was her chance to say goodbye. Before her tears turned into sobbing, Cara managed to whisper, "Goodbye Robert. I love you."

She started to move into the aisle behind him as he passed, but a woman gently pulled her arm and held her back. Everyone left the path through the center of the room open.

Robert used a chair to step up and then lie down in his glass coffin. He put his hands on his chest, and closed his eyes. A few sobs broke the silence. Cara wiped tears from her face and reached for John's hand. Everyone watched and waited, for what, Cara had no idea . . . but she stayed.

From the center of Robert's chest, the Great Spirit of the Eagle climbed out and perched on the far side of the glass box, behind the body. Spreading its wings wide and flapping them three times, the Great Eagle let out an ear-piercing screech. Cara and a few others covered their ears.

The Great Eagle brought its wings back in, stared straight ahead and waited. The room fell silent.

Slowly, the head of another bird emerged from Robert's chest. The Spirit of a Crow emerged to perch on the closer edge of the glass. Flapping its wings, it let out three caws. People applauded and cheered.

The Great Spirit of the Eagle opened its wings once again, lifted up and took flight through the clearing that everyone had left in the center of the room. The tips of its wings touched or went through some of the people in line, making them cry out in joy and raise their arms.

It flew the length of the room, out the door, into the hallway, then turned upwards and flew through the ceiling.

The Spirit of the Crow flapped its wings and lifted itself from the glass box. It circled over the crowd three times and cawed. Then it too, flew through the human passageway to follow the Eagle out, up, and away.

Cara had been holding her breath. When the Spirit of the Crow flew out of sight, she gasped and let out a cheer with the rest of the room. John laughed and joined in the clapping. The steel drums started to play again, and dancing once more animated the room.

Cara couldn't join them. Her legs felt like jelly. She was so overwhelmed with what she had just witnessed, she was surprised she was still upright.

She looked at John, smiled and said, "Take me home."

"He made me promise I would," John said, and winked.

One of the great joys of editing is finding someone who is just starting out, and is already so completely on fire that all you wanna do is hold the door open, and let the quality speak for itself.

This is only Leslianne's second published story. Her first—in Shock Totem #2—made me seek her out at the very last minute, sneakily suspecting that she might have Bizarro star potential. And I stand by my intuition.

24 hours later, she sent me this freshly-minted treasure. "But looking for the lost heart was something I'd had in my head for a while," she says. "I think anyone who's been out in the dating world probably knows the feeling."

I Fall to Pieces
by Leslianne Wilder

I'm wearing a banker. I should have taken him off, sloughed the trimmed chest hair and frameless glasses to the floor and just been naked with her, but I'm shy sometimes. I know, even if she's only what she appears to be, that she deserves better than I can give her right now.

But I kiss her. I put my teeth and my fingers everywhere she asks, and I think she likes it. We drink scotch someone gave her for a birthday two years ago, the last time she ever spoke to them. I apologize for the stains on her couch. She says it doesn't matter, but I can see she's bothered, so I kiss her again. She's an intermediate level chess champion. She has trophies. Most of the food in her refrigerator is expired.

"I want to be so much more than I am," she says. I don't think she meant for me to hear, but I put my arm around her and kiss her forehead anyway. We're two warm points in the artificial chill of her apartment, things in a refrigerator. We'll go bad more slowly here than we would out in the warm June nights, but we won't last forever.

She runs a hand down the raised scar on my sternum.

"Surgery," I say. She doesn't question the story any more than she did the name.

When she falls asleep, I open her chest. I pin the flaps of her skin to the couch sides, and she looks like an orchid. I could pollinate her diaphragm. The inside of her is twisted tight. She's all gristle under the skin, and she moans too high when I pluck it, out of tune. I wonder if I could be happy here, all through the night, playing the strings inside her, making the nightmare music.

But no. Her heart is such a tiny thing, brown and dingy and wrinkled. It puffs up for half a second before it shrivels again. She only has one heart, and it isn't mine. Staying now would feel empty. I reach between her ribs and scrape up a little of the ethereal to give to the Mendicant, then I pin her closed again. I lick the wound and hold her until she breathes even again. Then I leave two hundred dollars and a note apologizing for the couch.

When I am out onto the street, I take the banker off and throw his skin in the trash.

I was naked as the face of God on the surface of the water. She was a heaven of ice above and fire below, and salt on my tongue in between them as I licked away the shape of her. For all I knew we were creating a world. Something new and beautiful.

"I'll show you mine," she whispered, "if you show me yours."

I cracked my ribcage back and let her touch the fluttering muscle. I let her hold it in both her cool, smooth hands.

I made love to her. It was the last time I saw my heart.

The Mendicant is splayed on the ceiling when I find him. His bare hands and feet hold him in place and a pale membrane like chicken skin nictates across his eyes. His suit is too small for his long body. He has naked wrists and ankles.

"Hello, Tinman," he says. I show him my hand without speaking, and he slides down the wall and licks the essence of soul from under my fingernails. For a moment he is the intermediate chess champion. His eyes squeeze close in junkie ecstasy.

There's a haze in the room that burns my eyes, and the wallpaper is yellow, charred around the edges. There is no furniture, only donation boxes, styrofoam cups inscribed with "please," monks' bowls, and little Christmas cauldrons hung from tripods. Gifts balance on all these things: cigarettes, cushions, coins and dollar bills, skulls and grave dust, books of prayer. Some of the boxes have padlocks, and they rattle when you hold them in the corner of your eye. "You said my heart would try to come back to me, that it would be drawn back. But it hasn't ever been. It's just been lonely people, one after another."

The Mendicant lolls his head until it rocks against his shoulder. "Did you hear the one about Buddha and the dead boy's mother? He said he'd bring back her son when she could fill a bowl with one grain of rice from every family who'd never lost a treasured one."

"That's no help." I kick a box to punctuate my point, then recoil when it screams like a child, and begins to weep and call a woman's name. I wonder what advice someone holds in trade for that. I wonder if it was worth what they had to give up.

The Mendicant's eyes close from four sides down to black periods in his face. "You going to cry out a flood to wipe away the sins of everyone, Tinman? There's no room for you on the boat. You could take a dozen hearts, and ribs besides, but you keep chasing one that isn't coming back. You could find it, if you tried, but you never trust."

"I looked!" I say again. Every night for years, I've pinned open lovers like a mortician. No one's brought me what I've been looking for.

When the Mendicant speaks again, his words have the electric shock of obvious truth. My muscles twitch and my mouth tastes like blood and pennies. "Every part of you but your damn mind knows how to find what you're looking for."

She could change her shape. She could be moonlight one minute, then a stockbroker the next. We played. We dressed each other up in flesh- embarrassing, exotic, silly, poignant. I was a cripple for her, and she was one of those sad railroad clowns, too thin for her patched purple pants. I was a woman stitched into fashion model perfection with gold wire that glinted when I moved. She was a soldier amputee. I was a black cat under the full moon. She was Harpo Marx.

I never trusted anyone the way I trusted her then. I told her all my secrets. I taught her every magic I knew. I lied. I pretended I could spin straw into gold for spoiled miller's daughters. I wanted to impress her.

When I woke up without my heart, I did not miss it more than her. It has taken me a long time to get my priorities straight again.

I want to be whole.

I am wearing a boy on the edge of adulthood, working fast food and enjoying pretending to hate my life, when the idea comes to me. It's only my mind that cannot find my heart, that keeps me anchored in my routines, that blinds me to what my eyes should know to see. The answer, then, is obvious.

I throw my hat into the frier. The hisses and angry yells are like fireworks and confetti in my mind. I slide across the counter and sprint out the door. I grin so hard it hurts the raw, red pimples on my borrowed face. I come to the park by the river, and I take my clothes off. I throw my shoes and my regulation shirt into the trees. My skinny, spotted disguise draws giggles from picnickers, and it makes me smile. A policeman comes to tell me I cannot do this, but he stops when I break my fingers off and throw them into the river. The stump of my palm oozes and I break it off to offer it to him. He backs away. He prays to God. He calls for backup. I hurl the hand into the bushes with all my might. I pull my arm and my legs from their sockets. There is a dump truck coming. I try to throw my leg into its bin and miss. It rolls into a storm drain. I catch it with the other, and it rumbles off down the shaded street. I put my thumb behind my eyes one at a time and throw them to the birds. Parts of me spread out in every direction.

I am one whole. I will find myself again. Every piece will seek out those closest to it, and surely one of them must find my heart.

When all the people have run in terror, and I am nothing but a mind, I wrap myself in a squirrel, and join the symposium of the park. I meditate on acorns and the generosity of litters.

Everything else is in the hands of the universe.

I tried to steal a heart once, when I could no longer stand the empty silence of still blood. I found a carriage horse whose owner had left it to woo tourists back to the velvet of his seats. The horse let its head hang. There was no grass, no herd, no freedom to run, no shade where it was allowed to stop and rub itself against a tree. I thought at the time it would be an act of mercy to take its heart. Perhaps it would die, or maybe without a heart it would turn into an automobile, and I would have liked to see that.

I waited until I was sure no one was looking, then I knelt beneath the horse and reached my hands into its chest. I wound my way through the viscera, between the thick, heavy spars of bone. It was a fine heart, the size of a cat, and thumping slow and steady, stately and foreign as a waltz. It was, I thought, a dependable heart.

But when I looked back I saw the animal down on its knees, with tears flowing from behind its blinders. The heart in my hands pulled back to it in an invisible tide of desperation.

I couldn't. I gently replaced the organ and stroked the animal's head until the crying stopped. Only a monster could ask any living thing to go on without a heart. One such as that deserved to have no heart at all.

I see a girl in my park one day. Her eyes are vacant, and her fingers are on backwards. When she opens her mouth, her teeth are wrong. All of the canines are in the front, like a bulldog, and she bites at the other children when they try to make fun of her. Sometimes she walks, sometimes she crawls on her knees through the grass. Sometimes she runs on all fours like a hyena. She is wearing a dirty dress that doesn't fit her, but it's hardly her fault. All those pieces finding their way together never had a mind to guide them.

I take a moment to look at what I am when I am undirected. The girl scratches without social regard. I think if I had had a hand in making her I would be deeply embarrassed, but knowing that I scattered her to the animals and the elements and yet she pulled herself together into what could pass for an unfortunate human makes me very proud of myself.

I am wearing a goose today, and I fly down in front of her. I spread my wings, honk, and hiss. The misshapen girl throws her arms around me. I can feel the beat of life inside the uneven bars of her rib cage. The joy is better than flying.

I have it all back. I can be whole.

I see the shadow that trails behind her. There is a woman there, and her face is close enough to the monstrous little girl that she could be her mother, but far enough to be beautiful as well. She has short hair and earrings shaped like lightning bolts. I waddle in front of my twisted body and my errant heart and I hiss at her. She's followed me here. My heart races behind me, and the first thought on my mind is: did she come back because she loves me? Is this a game to her? Some courtship I misunderstood? Did she merely jump at some new opportunity to hurt me?

"Hello again," she says. She has teeth and eyes like a fox. "I missed you."

I've lied to so many people. I've let them assume things I knew were nothing but hope and kite string. I'm a trickster, and I can spot tricks. Except with her. She is a smooth and perfect wall, and the only way to know whether it hides a garden or a prison is to climb it.

My horrible little body hugs me close. The heart I looked so long for beats hard against my feathers. I waddle away from it, and I lay my head in her hand. She strokes me, and it fills an emptiness beyond fingers, toes, stomach, or heart.

Behind me, the little girl cries. I'd like to comfort her.

But I've found what I was looking for.

As a kid, the astounding Dr. Seuss was the first Bizarro author and artist I ever encountered. And no creator before or since has ever marked me harder.

So I can't even tell you how happy I am to bring you this whimsically psychotic charmer by my own sweet first-born daughter, told entirely in the awesome Seussian rhythms I was lucky enough to be able to pass on.

"My head was just feeling so outside of itself," she says, "that turning it into a children's story seemed like the best possible way to make it fun, and get it out of my skull." And that's precisely what happened.

Brain Monster
by Melanie Skipp

There is a little animal
He lives inside my head
One day I tried to speak with it
And this is what we said:

"Hello," I use my inside voice
Although it sounds insane
"What and who and why are you
That lives so near my brain?"

"An imp, a gnat, a hinkypunk
A demon if you wish
I like the heat and dark of it
The meat that smells of fish"

"My God!" I cry in great alarm
"How did this come to be?
If you keep feasting on my mind
What will become of me?"

"I came in while your dreams went
bad
All snug inside your bed
And when I've feasted to my full
I fear you will be dead."

The monster spoke inside my mind
As loud as thoughts can be
It hummed and laughed a wicked laugh
All snide and demony

"There must be something I can do
Or something I can say
A way to keep my brain intact
Or make you go away"

My face went pale, my body hot
And frothing through a grin
I tore my hair and ran at walls
My world began to spin

"Don't fight me now, you won't
succeed
Your motor skills are mine
I have control of every move
I hate to hear you whine

"Now get this straight, my little bitch
I like the way you taste
To eat until there's nothing left
Seems such an awful waste"

I'd stay alive and grow my brain
The 100 cells a day
He'd use my form to play his games
And in my head he'd stay

It's been a year or so, I think
He won't allow much thought
I've killed and fucked and tortured men
And finally got caught

Oh God, please make this nightmare end
Please give me back my soul
Looks like I'm getting 10 to life
This does not please the troll

The next few days will be a blur
My mind digesting fast
He'll eat until I decompose
We'll both be free at last

Let me speak and clap my hands
And give me my last days
I masturbate and hug a guard
We go our separate ways

Road Warrior Werewolves versus McDonaldland Mutants . . . post-apocalyptic fiction has never been quite like this.

They call themselves the Warriors, their enemies call them the Bitches. They are a gang of man-eating, motorcycle-riding, war-hungry werewolf women, and they are the rulers of the wasteland.

A century after the fall of civilization, only one city remains standing. It is a self-contained utopian society protected by a three-hundred-foot-high steel wall. The citizens of this city live safe, peaceful lives, completely ignorant to the savagery that takes place beyond the walls. They are content and happy, blindly following the rules of the fascist fast food corporation that acts as their government. But when Daniel Togg, a four-armed bootlegger from the dark side of town, is cast out of the walled city, he soon learns why the state of the outside world has been kept secret. The wasteland is a chaotic battleground filled with giant wolves, mutant men, and an army of furry biker women who are slowly transforming into animals. Trapped on the wrong side of a war zone, Daniel Togg makes new friends and new enemies, while uncovering the mysteries of the people living in the wasteland and how they came to be there.

Including 45 illustrations by the author, *Warrior Wolf Women of the Wasteland* is an epic bizarro tale of dehumanization, gender separation, consumption, and violent sexual awakenings. A fast-paced post-apocalyptic adventure in the vein of *The Road Warrior,* featuring a very unique werewolf mythology.

Warrior Wolf Women of the Wasteland
by Carlton Mellick III
Available on Amazon.com

Sometimes it's not what happens in the story, but what happens to your brain while you're reading it that's important. In those cases, it's less a story than a mind-altering substance you ingest with your eyes.

By that standard, "Impresorium" plays more at the Naked Lunch end of the scale, piling on the contradictory what-ifs until the only thing you're sure of is that shit just got weird in a hurry, and you could spend your whole life trying to sort it out.

And as with the Burroughs: GOOD LUCK WITH THAT!

Impresorium
by D. Harlan Wilson

Drunk on cheap champagne, a man and a woman exchange blows in a hotel elevator; one complains of being deeply unsettled with their relationship while the other lays blame on mere grumpiness and possibly fatigue. Accusations of baldness follow critiques of poorly manicured feet. Voices ascend into the realm of elements.

The elevator stops on the xth floor and a Certified Elevator Technician enters the chamber. He says there's a problem with the circuit breaker, but before he can remove the control panel, the man and the woman implicate him, charging him with an impossible task. Resolute, the CET pulls at the fabric of a loose-fitting uniform, analyzing it, closely, as if the fabric might somehow possess knowledge. But he has already lost his wits . . . The CET disappears into a ceiling panel and falls upwards into the elevator shaft, searing his palms whenever he grips the cables . . .

The man's sciatic nerve gives out. He has to lie down. His lower spine twitches like an insect, prompting him to cry out. The woman shows little sympathy; in fact, she becomes more enraged, threatening to leave him, and then she attacks him with a stiletto, puncturing the flesh of his cheeks, his flailing arms . . .

The elevator stops on the xth floor and a protectorate of suicide artists inundate the chamber. They are underwater. With overwhelming resolve, they hold intricate shark knives to their necks, threatening to produce their masterworks as they paddle in violent circles. The woman attempts to join their ranks. She fails, and the man flips onto his side, reaches for the control panel and pushes a button.

The elevator stops on the xth floor and the doors slide open and the suicide artists flow out of the chamber, knocking over chairs and lampstands and idle bellhops.

"Bald-*ing*," says the man, climbing to his feet. But the walls don't have railings and he has nothing to grab onto and he falls down again, pushing out his chest and clawing at his backside. Blood escapes from trivial wounds. The woman lights a cigarette and examines the ember before breathing in the content. She holds it in until her eyes roll back into her head. She faints, knees opening into a fearsome wingspan. Her lounge dress rips from heel to bra and, for a moment, somehow, they manage to roll around like lovers, envisioning themselves in precarious but inspiring contexts, where the engines of futurity rev and hum, and moths dance in the light of dire afterworlds, and windblown mannequins strike aggrieved poses . . .

The elevator stops on the xth floor and somebody hurls a mannequin into the chamber. It hits the far wall and breaks apart like porcelain. The woman observes all of the bodyparts and becomes paranoid, frightened. The man consoles her; he tells her not to look at it, tells her it's going to be all right; he stands halfway up and tries to hug her, but the pinched nerve flattens him. Neck corded, he arches his back and fumbles with his spine.

The elevator stops on the xth floor. A concierge paces back and forth in the hallway. Aghast, he signals a cleaning crew with a walkie-talkie. It takes awhile for them to get there. Distinguished by an impeccably groomed beard of fire, the concierge assures the man and the woman that they will be given vouchers for any inconvenience. He places two fingers on the doorslot, keeping the elevator at bay. He looks at the floor. He grinds his jaw. Sparks fly from the beard and turn to airy flecks of ash.

Beleaguered by useless industrial equipment, the cleaning crew takes away the sordid remnants of the mannequin. Accidentally they try to take away the woman. The concierge apologizes and offers her an additional voucher. All vouchers may be collected from the front desk at both party's earliest convenience . . .

The elevator stops . . . A man and a woman stare at the ceiling. The lights flicker. They continue to flicker. The man studies himself. He studies himself with greater acuity. He lifts a finger and taps the ceiling. It seems to work, the ceiling. The woman is skeptical. She lights a cigarette. Smoke leaks from her nostrils in agitated curls. The man doesn't know what to do. Cables creak nefariously. Voices descend into the chamber. The cosmos glints. The woman suspects a trap. She expresses herself. The man advises against expression. Expression incites conflict. The woman faints. She awakens immediately, stands, repositions her shoulderblades, and faints again. The man studies himself. Something is wrong. Something isn't working. The woman faints again despite being unconscious. The man lies on the floor beside her, mimicking her. He rests a cheek against the carpet. He closes his eyes and tries to faint. He can't. Scenes from a silent film race across his mind's screen. He can't read the subtitles. He opens his eyes and looks at the carpet. He admires the pattern. He wonders how it was conceived, and by whom. The lights go out. The man doesn't know what to do. There is a moment of raw anxiety during which the man imagines his own death. Inconceivable. Contemptible. Illimitable. He crawls atop the woman. He tries not to crush her and listens to her breathe in the darkness. Gently, rhythmically, their bodies rise and fall, rise and fall.

Right about the time that Marc and I began writing The Emerald Burrito of Oz, we were invited to participate in a gargoyle anthology. And being who we are, we eschewed the whole gothic cathedral motif, and set the crazy fucker on Mars instead.

It's not the most optimistic glimpse of the future ever presented, but it does offer up one glimmer of hope: the notion that, someday, The Weekly World News will return in all its glory, and be spread to other planets.

As the greatest of all supermarket tabloids—and Bizarro down to its ingrown yellow toe- nails—I think I speak for both of us when I unequivocally declare it the fount from which this story sprung. (That, and Frank Zappa's classic anthem for losers, "Wind Up Working in a Gas Station.")

Now Entering Monkeyface
by John Skipp and Marc Levinthal

1.

It's always tough to meet a legend. Tough for the legend, and tough for you.

Frank knows this, knows it all too well. He remains, however, vastly unconsoled by the understanding. He is soaring through the infinite in a low-budget space shuttle—the interstellar equivalent of a Greyhound bus— in the company of sixty-seven painfully ripe- smelling strangers. (He has counted them. More than twice.)

Moments before, the captain had advised them all to direct their attention out the window to their left. Suddenly, they're all crowded on his side, looking out the greasy windows at the surface of Mars, and one of its most famous landmarks.

Said landmark is also his destination.

He squints at it till his stomach hurts.

"It doesn't look anything like a goddam monkey face," Frank mumbles at last, as the shuttle burns the last few thousand miles to the spaceport.

"Sure it does!" yells Bradley, a cute little freckle-faced kid whom Frank will despise till the day he dies. "Can'cha see his sungoggles?"

"*No.*"

"I still can't see it, honey," Bradley's oversized mother complains, clutching her rumpled *Weekly World News*. Monkeyface is on the cover, next to the headline LOVE SECRETS OF MARTIAN HEAD! So, Frank notes, is one whole hell of a lot of airbrush work.

But this woman is that *special* kind of stupid: the kind that believes that spinach causes cancer, or that Bat Boy and Lisa Marie Presley's daughter gave birth to Corey Feldman in a time machine. She has also been a monumental pain in the ass, from the moment they cut loose of Earth's ravaged atmosphere: foghorn snore, sulpherous bowels, voice that sounds the way it feels when you bite down hard on tinfoil.

The woman leans closer, unspeakably pungent, accidently elbowing Frank in the head. "*Ow!*" says Frank, but no excuse me's are forthcoming. The kid yells something—

he *always* yells—about why can't you use your mamagination. Frank, in turn, blissfully mamagines cramming the little bastard right back into his mother's womb. Then he leans forward—far as he can, away from her armpit—and renews his attempts to see.

Could be any number of things, he thinks, turning his head sideways and back. Could be, like, a lady's shoe, or a boomerang stuck in a pile of dogshit. Fucking idiots. It's like seeing Jesus on a tortilla. You can see anything on anything, for crissake!

Then again, it's still hard to make out something even a mile across from this high up. And judging from some of the oohs and ahhhs, *somebody* besides Bradley must be seeing this thing.

Frank gives up, disgusted, unstraps himself, and cautiously stands before the throngs. "Stay outta my goddam seat," he warns the adorable moppet; then he elbows his way down the corridor to the head, grabbing seats when he can, pulling himself along.

He's thankful for small favors: he only has to piss. And he's starting to feel a little less green than he has for the past two weeks. Mercifully, the perpetual dry-heaves stopped about a week out; but the nausea has lingered, like the stale puke smell that hangs around the shuttle.

He closes the door, makes a grab for one of the paper dick-cups and attaches it to the vacuum hose. As he fastens it over his spout, the unnerving grabbing sensation gives way to relief as the pee drains out of his bladder. It almost makes him happy.

The last time he remembers "happy" was the day Snid emailed and told him about the opening at his gas depot: somebody waiting in line for a lichen-dusting gig finally got called.

"Mars needs Women . . . and Men!" So the lame MarsCorp slogan proclaimed. MarsCorp needed bodies: that was the truth of the matter. Therefore, MarsCorp checked your pulse, ran you through the Disease-O-Meter, and didn't ask you too many more questions. Bingo.

Frank could have gotten into the Terraform program any number of ways, but he waited to do it Snid's way. Snid had a dream (translation: scam), which he refused to discuss with Frank until he got there; but Snid guaranteed that it would turn them both into rich men, and fast.

True, Snid's record didn't bode well for the future. There was the chinchilla farm, the AMWAY thing, and of course the big Baldness Cure fiasco: the one that had sent Snid on his merry-all-the-way to Fuel Depot 807, Cydonia, Mars, in the first place.

Still, Frank had a feeling about this one. Snid liked to shoot his mouth about everything, to everyone; and the fact that he didn't this time made Frank wonder if his pal hadn't finally struck gold after all.

He remembers thinking, as he closed the door for the last time on his little rat hole apartment—beating impending eviction by mere hours—what some asshole had once said . . .

. . . that even a busted clock tells the right time once a day. Or something.

That moment, that feeling, was sort of like happy. This, on the other hand, is not. He spends a moment in the spider-cracked mirror, remembering precisely that fact.

"Yuck," he says, surveying his thin, greasy salt-and-pepper hair, his haggard complexion in the ugly halogen light. Frank is fifty-five years old, and all he's got to show for it is paunch and wrinkles, creaks and complaints (plus a crappy little suitcase, the clothes on his back, and handful of pocket change, diminishing fast).

Truth is, life has not been kind to Frank. Every dream he ever had fell apart, drifted off, was brutally dismembered, or—worst of all—never even came close. He is so far past mere "disappointment" that the concept invokes bland nostalgia in him.

He thinks to himself: hey, I mean, here it is! The glorious Future of Humanity! Soaring to distant galaxies; reclaiming hope for the children of a dying planet. It's a golden age, alrightee.

And where the fuck am I?

I'm in the reeking commode of a ValuJet shuttle, trying to make sure I don't piss all over myself.

He waits a moment for the last drops to get sucked off before he removes the cup and shoves it in the waste receptacle. Even so, when he takes it off, a tiny golden globule escapes from his penis, does a merry slow caper around the toilet cubicle. The one serious design flaw in the human body, he thinks. Besides nostrils and sinuses.

And everything else.

2.

The drive from the spaceport takes about seven and a half hours. It doesn't look much different to Frank than parts of Nevada he's driven through. The one big difference is that, if you got out to stretch your legs or take a whiz, your lungs would be in for a big, bad surprise. Not to mention that it's a bit chilly out there without your woolies—gets to be 95 below sometimes.

Of course, Bemy the driver tells him in clipped Bombay English, parts of the year are nice and warm; you could go out with a mask on and almost think you were back home. Almost.

The pressurized bus rolls through spectacular vistas of mountain ranges that rival the Himalayas, seem to poke out through the atmosphere (as Bemy tells him, some actually do). These are punctuated, on a regular basis, by mind-numbing stretches of desolation. Bemy doesn't have much to say about that.

Frank doesn't mind; he's just relieved to be free of all those people. (He's also slightly alarmed by just how much of the smell was *him*.) He spends a lot of time with his feet up on the seat, looking around, thinking too much about too little, slipping sporadically into alpha state. A long stretch of that goes by, and he almost dreams.

"Getting close now," Bemy says at last, rousing Frank out of a half-doze.

"How the hell can you tell?" Frank says, blinking his eyes.

Out of nowhere, a sign jumps up over the horizon:

FUEL DEPOT 807 — 3 KILOMETERS

And then, looming up right behind it, a gigantic, leering hand-painted chimpanzee dressed like an Egyptian, bearing the legend:

NOW ENTERING MONKEYFACE
POP. 12
MYSTERIOUS CYDONIAN ARTIFACTS
GIFT SHOP AHEAD
VISIT ANGRY RED'S SALOON

"Sonofabitch." Frank gets that sinking feeling. He knows Snid's handiwork when he sees it.

Bemy's grinning ear to ear. "Think I'll get a drink or three while I'm here."

"Sonofabitch."

"Might buy one of those little monkey heads for my kid."

Frank's got his head in his hands. "Fuck!"

"Maybe one of those Monkey T-shirts."

3.

His name is Sidney; but for some arcane reason, lost in the mists of time, he has always been known as Snid. No matter where he goes, no matter what new community he finds himself in, people who started out calling him Sidney eventually find themselves calling him "Snid."

Snid has not aged well. Ten years younger than Frank, but you wouldn't know it now. He has half as many teeth as he had at age one. He claims it's something in the water. Frank's ecstatic about that.

Snid takes a swig off his seventh straight Pabst. His Adam's apple bobs in his scrawny throat like a Pez dispenser locked on semiautomatic. He's nearly bald on top, but hanging on to his mohawk, which means that there's a thin strip of baby-fine whisp streaking dead center down the length of his dome, and then a scraggy little strag-tail in the back.

It's the most retarded fashion statement Frank has ever seen, but the horror doesn't quite end there. Snid's tattoos, done as a teen back in the year 2001, are no longer even legible. They just look like bad ink smears. He's got them all over his body, but he still wears his vest wide open—tattered tie-dye, with fringe—and his beer gut poking out through the breach like a mange-ridden medicine ball.

"Anyhow," Snid continues, "why am I not surprised that you think it doesn't look like a monkey face?" He shows all his teeth in an enormous grin. "Because it doesn't." He wags his finger in front of his face like a conductor's baton. "Because it DOES INT."

Snid takes a quick toke, and without exhaling, leans forward with a crazed conspiratorial leer. "Because the U.N. Forces in the Black Shuttles came up here and…" he exhales, "…CHEMICALLY ALTERED the outside of the Monkeyface.

"They didn't fuck with the insides. No no no. Because that's where all the shit is, man.

"That's where all the shit is."

Frank stares at him, and Snid stares back.

"Y'see 'em coming out of there sometimes, man." Snid passes him the joint.

Frank looks at the joint, looks back up at Snid.

"You're a fucking idiot, dude. Has anyone ever told you that?"

Snid makes the half-panicky, all-defensive snivelface. It's a face Frank knows all too well. The pale arms flap, smudgy wattles nearly audible.

"There's nothing . . . " He falters. "I'm not saying anything that's not . . ." Again. He sucks in breath, eyeballs ballooning in moist entreaty. "There's PROOF . . .!"

"How much did those T-shirts cost you, anyway? What made you think you would sell more than one of those things a week, anyway?"

Snid attempts a weak response. Frank is not in the mood to hear it.

"Hey," he says. "Fuck this, fuck you, fuck the fucking monkey face, alright?"

He storms out of the room, Snid stunned into silence.

And then it's just Frank, in the parking lot, surveying the grandeur that is Depot 807. He lights a cigarette, just to commemorate the event.

There's a whole lot of Martian dirt. A few crummy hovels. A hot dog stand. All of it's enclosed in a terraformed bubble, maybe thirty acres square, color of an Army blanket. There's also a road that runs straight down the middle of town. It ends in duel airlocks. They might as well be Hell's gates.

Although, actually, he feels more like a tenant in a roach hotel.

He thinks about Earth, about how depressing it had become. Wearing breathmasks on the streets. Mutant rats. The whole ordeal. Suddenly, in retrospect, Earth doesn't seem all that bad. There was a vibrancy to it. Mostly terror, but *still* . . .

Frank finds himself suddenly longing for White Castle wormburgers, teenage violence, the occasional toddler in flames. He pines for the constant sirens, the religious mania that took off around Millennium, the endless holovision bullshit, the bottomless corruption of home.

A tear wells in his eyes. It's almost embarrassing. If he had any pride left, he'd kick his own ass. But that commodity seems as far away as the ruins of Grauman's Chinese, on that island of rubble once known as L.A.

Something opens up inside of Frank: a canyon at his core that is screaming to be filled; a now-accessible receptivity, yawning and yearning for meaning. He feels a sob well up as well, chokes it back, then says fuggit and lets them come.

They do. He's too numb to bawl—too completely in shock—so the sobs are like seizures from an engine utterly drained of oil or lube. He takes it as long as he can.

And then he can't take it no more.

Calling upon faith that he has never once possessed, he finds himself ridiculously praying to God. Face uplifted. Hands in the air. Desperately praying that there's an upside to destiny; praying for a solitary sign that this is not, oh please please please, the single worst move he has ever made in his whole dumb goddam stupid fucking life.

As if in answer, a mutant rat scurries across the street.

"Oh, good," he says.

And then Snid is there, still holding out the joint, like some kind of sacrificial offering. He pats Frank on the back with his free hand and says, "Swear to God, dude. This place is gonna be a gold mine."

An ugly toothpick woman appears in the street. Snid waves at her. She snubs him cold. "That's Sara," he says. "She's one red-hot woman. Won't be long before you can afford her love."

Frank doesn't have the strength to shake his head.

"Did I mention," Snid inquires, "that I'm running for mayor?"

4.

Nothing changes, except that he's here. One truck rolls by about once every two hours, at least this time of year. Frank sits in the gift shop, tapping his toes, waiting for a trucker to come up, stick his retinas in front of his scanner, and ask for a pack of chewing gum or a slurpie or maybe where can a guy get laid around here?

Well, there are in fact four female humans here that run a kind of whorehouse/laundromat, but personally, I'd go right across the hall to this hemisphere's largest collection of holoporn for your wanking enjoyment, if in fact you actually want to enjoy yourself, pal. But as long as you're here, can I interest you in a fine plastic replica of a reconstruction of the original Monkeyface? Or one of these cute little stuffed monkeys in an Egyptian getup? Or how bout one of these "I've been to the Monkeyface" T-shirts?

Not me, he thinks, not in a million fucking years. I'll sit in this goddam place, I will take the money, I will live down the humiliation of ending up working in a gas station on Mars, but

I'll be damned if I'll pimp or hawk these stupid Made-in-Taiwan pieces of shit for any reason.

He glances over at a row of Monkey-toys against the far wall.

Frank wonders what would possess a man to take his hard-earned cash—money that he could have saved against his old age—and plow it back into this crap. The little simian heads look as though they are almost nodding their agreement.

Am I right, monkeyheads, am I right?

You are right, they seem to agree. Their faces beam in total blissful acceptance.

Frank is suddenly skeptical. Are you agreeing, my little friends, or are you in fact mocking me? Are you mocking me? For I am not a man to be trifled with. I can stand so much, and then . . .

A trucker is standing in front of the register, face mask pulled up over his wooly cap. He gives Frank a funny look before gazing up into the retina scanner. "Fill it on fifteen."

The register dings, and the monitor on Frank's side scrolls the driver's ID and credit info.

"All set," Frank says. "And have a *really nice day*, okay?"

The trucker dons his mask again, though he doesn't really need to; and in a moment Frank hears the northern airlock whoosh as it cycles. Another customer, Frank thinks, but nobody comes. Evidently, it was somebody leaving.

A few minutes later he hears the faint whine of the truck's hydrogen turbines as it rolls away. Once again, he is immersed in the ancient Martian silence.

"Fuck this. Computer! Music. 'Highway to Hell'."

The computer complies. The antique strains of AC/DC, headbanging across from nearly a century ago, rise and kick away the oppressive quiet.

Frank always did enjoy the old stuff, never could go for the Ninja Gothic Karaoke Disco or what ever the hell they were shoving down people's throats this week. That's what he'd been trying to do back at the Dung Club, but nobody was buying it. Nobody liked the live acts he was booking. (Of course nobody really knew how to play rock and roll anymore—sure they could copy, but the *feel*—it was a lost art. Fucked him out of that job.)

But hey, look at these guys, he thinks. They seem to be enjoying it. The bobbing, spring-headed variety of monkeys rock sympathetically to the thudding kick drum. The stationary variety on the far wall seem to like it as well.

However, the Monkeyface plastic replicas appear to be on the fence, not sure whether or not it would be proper to admit to a pleasurable sensation. Kind of a fart-holding face.

"What is *with* you fuckers?" he asks them out loud, annoyed by their gassy stoicism. "Don't know how to have a good time?"

The Monkeyfaces eye him—in fact, it seems like they're *all* just staring at him—and the effect is entirely unnerving. Little monkeyfaced gargoyles, hording some kind of secret. Withholding the facts.

Just like Snid's Black Shuttles . . .

"I gotta get outta here," Frank hears himself say. Truer words were never spoken. He thinks this, looking into those blank monkey eyes, and a chill wiggles through him, yanks him up on his feet.

There's a sign on the door. It says CLOSED, from where he's sitting. He walks over to it and flips it around. It's early afternoon on Mars. Snid will be pissed, but it's impossible to care.

"I gotta get outta here," he says again.

And then locks the door behind him.

5.

It looks alot like Ayer's Rock in Australia from this side. Bigger, though. It's a mile wide, and maybe a third as high. Frank's gotten used to the scale of things, like everyone on Mars does after a while, but this is still a majestic and lonely sight.

What he hasn't gotten used to is the solitude.

This, he guesses, is part of his therapy. Shortly after the feeble sun had cleared the horizon, he'd nabbed the settlement's Helsina 50, a kind of pressurized shopping cart on bubble-wheels, and rolled out over the plain down to the Face.

The Helsina is a cheap, dependable ATV; it's the Volkswagen Bug of Mars, and has made a few wiley Icelanders into rich men.

This particular ride is murder on Frank's hemorrhoids, and the torpid drone of the engine does not inspire confidence. The fear of being stranded twenty kilometers from Monkeyface-proper (with only his Mars-wear between himself and certain death) lurks in the back of his mind.

It looks less like a Monkeyface from close up than it had from space. Or a face of any kind, for that matter. It looks like a big rock. Twenty kilometers away to the southwest are more big, portentous rocks—"The City"— that probably look even less like what people believed they really were.

Snid said that "The City" was where Martians lived before they died out, and we showed up.

"What the hell am I doing out here?" Frank mutters to himself as he approaches the rough wall of the Face. He puts his gloved hand out to touch it, almost expecting some cosmic, magnetically encoded knowledge to take possession of him and impart the mystic wisdom of the universe. But it behaves pretty much like a rock the whole time. He takes his hand away and looks up the side, into the pale red sky.

"Well," he says to no one in particular, "that was great. What a fucking waste of time."

He smacks his hands against one another and starts walking back to the Helsina.

He thinks he hears something.

Of course, he knows right away that it's stupid. There is no one around for twenty kilometers in any direction. But still, every time he starts to walk again, he (imagines) he hears it, out of the corner of his ear: a rumbling, a hum, a ringing. It buggers description, partly because it isn't there (he knows), and partly because it is an alien thing, almost a non-sound. A carrier wave for some kind of zeitgeist to be decoded somewhere in his hindbrain.

"Oh, and what exactly are you being told, Mr. Radiobrain?" he asks himself.

Things long hidden, the non-sound tells him.

And something happens.

He sees the plain transformed; an overlay appears, and all around him are people— well, not exactly people, but close enough— and they're doing people things. Well, not exactly people things—the mannerisms and movements are a little different—but basically, they are people. They're wearing clothing that looks vaguely Aztec, vaguely Egyptian. Like something out of an old Heavy Metal comic, he thinks; and some of them are rolling through in some kind of wheeled contraptions bellowing steam. Some walk right through him.

And some of them are wearing a kind of helmet, black priestly robes a-flutter in their wake, and Frank can see one of their faces for a moment. It looks him in the eyes, kind of looks through him . . .

. . . and it is, of course, at that precise moment that Frank feels himself leave his body: floating above it, airlifting like a skydiver film in reverse, up and up, while below him the whole of Martian civilization spreads out: "The City" a city, indeed, with suburbs that extend for miles in every direction . . .

. . . and at the center of the sprawl and bustle—looking more and more like some infinite, incredibly complex hi-tech ant farm, the higher he goes . . .

. . . he sees THE FACE.

He sees the Face, in all its glory; and he's amazed that he ever could have missed it before. It is not like the cover of the Weekly World News. *It is not like a monkey at all. Or maybe it is, but it's eons beyond. Like the difference between a paramecium and the Pope.*

The Face that looks up at him—mile wide, a third as high—is a carving of exquisite refinement and brain-devouring scale. An obviously superior civilization, calling out to some deity far beyond any half-baked, tepid vision cooked up by the mind of Man.

The Face is wise. The Face is calm. The Face knows all, and bides its time. The Face looks like it could just lay there forever. Completely content. Completely at peace.

And then it opens its eyes.

And that is when Frank begins to scream, mind wrenching as free from his soul as his soul has wrenched free of his body. Screaming as the mile-wide Face of Mars tears free from the soil and BEGINS TO RISE: enormous throat blowing up through the dirt, making way for miles of seismic displacement as shoulders almost too huge to imagine plow up from below. Pierce the surface. Rise up. Shrug off mountains that vanish in great plumes of dust, like a smoke machine roughly the size of Rhode Island kicking up a cloud cover for the resurgence of the King . . .

And then it's done. It's gone. It's all gone. He is back in his shoes, and the Martian world is silent. Frank staggers for a moment, catches himself.

And all he can say is "What the fuck was that?," the resonant edges of his words impossibly echoing off the sides of the Face.

Just a rock now. Nothing more.

Then he's dabbing at his helmet, as if he could catch the sweat now sluicing down his forehead, and he is thinking what was what? WHAT WAS WHAT? WHAT WAS WHAT? Well, let's see. Okay. I'm just out in the middle of nowhere, stressed out because I am working at a gift shop in the middle of Asswater, Mars, and I . . . had a little episode. That's all. Just . . . saw a tableau of the Lost Civilization of Mars, complete with Monkeyheads. That's all.

And he thinks about how Snid planted this shit in his head. And he thinks about how it means nothing at all. Maybe it's just something leaking in from the Martian atmosphere. Maybe he just needs to take a deep fucking breath. Maybe he's been drinking too much. Or not enough.

He looks at the rock. It's just a rock. That's all.

He climbs back into the Helsina.

And stomps on the pedal.

Hard.

6.

That night, he dreams.

And in the dream, he is sitting at the gift shop/gas station counter. He hears the rumble of the trucks, the tick and tocking of the clock. There are monkeyheads, yes. They are watching him closely.

He sees a shadow whisper past the front door.

Cold dread wells up inside him; but in the dream, he is terrible calm. He feels himself rise, move toward the door, and there's no fear in the gesture.

But there's fear in his heart.

He steps through the door, and the shadow is there: not a shadow at all, but a black cloaked figure. It is running toward the gas pumps, arms flowing up and out like wings; and now Frank hears somebody screaming. But only for a moment.

Frank comes closer. The shadow stands before a burly, squirting man: first the throat, then the belly, opened up and flowing heavy. Frank comes closer, watching the shadow reach one arm up inside the trucker's torso; watching the shadow root around, more than elbow-deep, in the chest cavity.

Watching the meat-plop of wet red innards, coruscating onto the trucker's boots and into the dirt.

As the shadow comes out with a still-beating heart.

And pops it into a bag.

There is more screaming now, from a bus that's parked at the second bank of pumps. Frank sees a pair of familiar faces, pressed against window glass. The trucker collapses, and the shadow takes off; closer now, Frank sees the Aztec/Egyptian motif of the garb. Weird golden cuniforms around the cowl that conceals the head; more ornate golden squiggles as piping for the cloak.

Frank feels himself running, trying to catch up with the shadow. The shadow rounds the front of the bus, races between the bus and the pumps. The bus driver ardently scratches his ass, clueless till seconds before the end. When it comes, Frank can't see it.

But then the shadow whips and turns.

And Frank sees the blade in its black-gloved hand. Sees the blood and the steel and the black matted sleeve. Then he looks in the eyes of the Martian before him. Black, impenetrable eyes. White, inpenetrable features.

The Martian shadow comes toward him, as the bus driver dies. Frank watches it all; but in the dream, he does not move. The Martian shadow walks right into his face.

Then passes through him.

As if he were not even there.

Frank turns. The Martian walks toward the front of the bus, where the door still hangs open. It steps inside. Frank follows, up the steps, past the vacant driver's seat, and walks the narrow course toward the back of the bus.

Beyond the shadow, he hears the howling of a woman and child.

It is at this point that Frank realizes he's walking through a dream. Up until that point, it had been too real. But somehow, recognizing the voices, he goes, hey! That's Bradley! And it all starts to turn.

Suddenly, it all begins to make dream-sense. He knows a wish-fulfillment fantasy when he sees one. And here's one now. Suddenly, he feels weirdly complicit. And not at all guilty.

While the shadow grabs Bradley and hacks off his head, Frank finds himself drawn to the cowering mother. She's as awful as he remembered her, and he loves her expression. It's completely terrified, and just as clueless as they come.

She flaps her arms as the shadow descends, but there's no self-defense in the gesture at all. She's just a fun bullseye target for some unconscious virtual role-playing game.

When she dies, it's not nearly bad enough.

Then the Martian shadow-icon moves back through Frank again, and he follows, away from the carnage. He almost feels like the game is running him, but dreams are strange, and he is consciously along for the ride.

The inside of Angry Red's is dank and hopeless as ever. Seven people are inside. That's half the population of 807, including Frank, who doesn't see himself seated at the bar.

The Martian-shadow hacks its way straight down the line of worthies: not pausing for hearts, but simply destroying. Severed neck. Torn-out lung. Gonads sliced up to jawline. A pair of eyeball piercings, and a slit throat for ballast. By the time Angry Red—a scrawny Irish/German mix—gets it up to find his handgun, his tongue is skewered to his pate: blade raking against the man's two front teeth as the point ventilates his hindbrain.

In dreamtime, the whole ordeal seems to take maybe a minute or less.

Now Frank is actively having some fun. Angry Red is a prick, and the rest are all drones. Not a soul worth preserving in the whole damn batch, including Sondra, who's the hottest of the laundry whores on hand.

Frank finds himself wanting to make whoopie with her corpse, absolved of the need to address her personal quirks with his social graces. But the shadow Martian stand-in is on the move, and he is moved to carry on in his voyeur's position.

So he finds himself racing down the street in pursuit, and the next stop is Sara's laundry love-in emporium. The washers and dryers are silent, but there's sound from above, and it's the base noise of heinous amour. Without a moment's hesitation, he races up the steps toward the second-floor brothel that houses, as it turns out, another half-dozen of Cydonia's finest.

They all die and die and die.

In his dream-head, he does the calculations. This leaves two, counting the absence of the one who just left. Lichen-dusting: a good call for whoever-the-fuck it was.

With a little time to spare, the Martian shadow goes over the victims.

Removing hearts, and bagging them.

Leaving very little left to be done.

But the fear returns to Frank as he follows the shadow back out onto the street, through the pluming Martian dust and toward the gas pump/gift shop fulcrum. There, he knows, the real Frank is just stupidly sitting around: waiting for the bus and truck to pay up and get out of here.

He finds himself thinking *oh no, oh no*; and he picks up his pace, but the shadow does, too. And he finds himself running, as the shadow takes off, and there's no way to make himself run fast enough.

He blows through the door, and all at once, he's in his chair.

And the shadow is standing directly before him. Seeing him now.

Seeing him clear.

Monkey boy, the shadow says. And Frank has nothing to say. *Monkey boy, we thank you for the hearts.*

Please deliver them unto me.

And Frank is rooted in his chair, watching a million years of perished wisdom patiently advance. He watches the face get closer, closer, from a yard to a foot to an inch.

In the dream, Frank intuits a subtle and ugly thing. Is amazed by its power. Is amazed by how far beyond all that he's known this dream seems to penetrate.

Frank feels himself lifting the bag. Feels the thump and the roll of the wet human hearts. They are rolling, from solid squirting here to spurting there.

All encased in the bag that he holds in his hand.

And then he sees the face of Snid, staring dumbstruck, and the dream starts to de-rezz. Sluicing light into the tangible darkness.

Reclaiming life, as it blows through the dream . . .

7.

...**and** suddenly, he's sitting in the chair behind the cash register, just as he had last seen himself; and there's Snid, precisely where the shadow had stood in the dream.

"Frank, jesus, don't hurt me . . ." Snid is saying; and Frank thinks, why would I want to hurt *you*?

Frank stands, and Snid backs away, cowering. "What's the deal?" Frank says.

And then Snid turns into the Shadow.

Frank blinks, looks at Snid, only Snid isn't there; and the walls start to shift from coal black to dull gray. It's like the dream is a colorless transparency, draping itself over the waking world.

Then Snid is back; and on the walls, the monkeyfaces are approving.

Frank continues to watch, fascinated, as different parts of Snid shift back and forth into Shadow. Shadow, then Snid, there long enough to repeat, "Don't hurt me . . . don't . . ."

Then that singsong, too, melts into the resonant carrier wave-song from the Cydonian plain.

Frank comes around the counter, puts his arms out to cowering Snid. "Of course I won't hurt you, you shithead . . ." he says . . .

. . . and then he sees the bag he's clutching in one of his own outstretched hand: paper and plastic, with dark brownish blood seeping through the soaked paper, pooling in the bottom against the white plastic.

The Shadow stops cowering and approaches Frank. Putting out its arms. Mirroring Frank.

Take it, the Shadow thinks at him. *Take your face, Monkeyman. Come take it, Monkeyking.*

And now the Shadow wears a face—sad, lovely flat simian face—and the coal black eyes pin him even as he approaches it to merge, to receive (he knows) his own true face.

As they press together, front to front, arms outstretched, they merge; and the resonant note ramps up to a crescendo that strangely twists back into Snid's tortured screams as Frank lets him drop, strides to the front door, popping yet another into the fresh bag of hearts.

His offering to the People.

He can hear them already, as he walks toward the southern exit of ghostly Depot 807. Can hear the cheers, in the ancient tongue, soon to be revived again.

They are cheering for him, for the next great champion.

The One Long-Awaited, finally back where he belongs.

"ALL HAIL MONKEYFACE!" they call out as one as he pauses, humbly, at the door.

"ALL HAIL MONKEYFACE!!!" they call out again, and he is nearly overwhelmed by the glory.

"ALL HAIL MONKEYFACE!!!" comes their delirious cry.

Then he opens the airlock, and lets in the sky.

The world has become an ever-more-painfully strident place, where emotional reaction trumps thoughtful response almost every chance it gets. Hard times make hard people, no matter how nice they think they are, and can even sometimes be.

That's why simplistic slogans are the bomb. They're easy to memorize, and chant in crowds, and parrot to others till they nearly pass for truth.

"I always drive behind folks with bumper stickers that are so emphatic and self satisfied," says JDO. "I wanted to write a story in which one had an actual effect." And so he's done, with this crunchy sonofabitch.

And A Wake Up
by J. David Osborne

Gershwin picked the bumper sticker out of its cage at a Flying J off I-35. The glossy laminate calmed his nerves, shot to hell from Dallas traffic. The clerk placed Gershwin's purchases in a plastic bag like a nurse dressing an old man.

He set the bag on his trunk and attached the sticker to the right side of his bumper, just above the tailpipe. He used his credit card to smooth the bubbles. From a few feet back, resting his shoulder on a gas pump, Gershwin nursed the two American vindications sixty-nining in his guts: the warm satisfaction that, through his beliefs, he could now separate himself from the herd, and the buttery goodness of a righteous purchase.

An hour later, Gershwin disengaged the cruise control and sank to sixty miles per hour to accommodate the two eighteen wheelers occupying both lanes. He turned down the radio so that God could hear him vent. He finished the last of his drink and threw it into the plastic bag, waving his arms like a conductor.

Nearly undetectable under the rumble of his high speeds, something in his car began to hum.

The trucks separated, the driver in the fast lane claiming a gradual win, and Gershwin slammed his foot the last few inches into the carpet and the car bucked forward and sped on. As he passed the truck drivers, his rage simmered to regret and he promised, next time, he'd stay zen.

That night Gershwin pulled into a motel just south of Oklahoma City. He told the night clerk that he liked her eye makeup. She slid him his key card and receipt. On his way out he held the door for an elderly Hispanic woman. Just before the door closed, he heard the clerk's voice change decibels to "foreigners and deaf people" volume, and feeling the need to help, walked back into the lobby and helped the clerk explain to the old woman that he had just rented the last room.

He reached into his backseat and took out a gift wrapped box. He popped his trunk and set his suitcase on the ground with the box and when he slammed it shut he noticed that his bumper sticker, which he had so carefully manicured earlier that day, had once again bubbled. After pressing against the imperfections with his credit card, he realized that the protrusions were not bubbles but rather, and he didn't believe himself when he thought it, muscles.

A moth flitted in the frail lamplight. He blinked several times, shook his head, and carried his belongings to his room.

Gershwin occupied the handicapped-accessible unit. He took a shower and fought the spell of dizziness brought on by the vast expanse of checkerboard tile. He ordered a John Wayne film on pay-per-view and fell asleep.

When he woke the next morning he changed the channel and watched the heads argue while he brushed his teeth. He turned in his key, ate, and pulled back onto the highway, fumbling with the radio for a news station.

The prairie dipped and bowed into rolling hills and old white men yelled on the radio. They espoused views. They passed judgments. Gershwin could hear the red in their faces; feel the spittle from their invective. He got so riled up that now even he could feel it: something was definitely humming in the back of his car.

He pulled off to the side of the road. He checked under the hood. He inspected the tires. He thought back to the last time he got his car detailed. He invented a face, some doe-eyed mechanic, and he hated that face for whatever they missed, whatever they did to fuck up his car, and as he hated his phantom, he heard the humming again.

Coming from the bumper.

He tried to rationalize what he saw. At first he thought he had hit an animal, a white snake, but no, it would have to have been a *pair* of white snakes.

The car hummed.

Clearing his head, Gershwin squatted over the blacktop and squinted at the bumper of his car. The sticker was still there, and it had grown a pair of muscular arms. Attached to the ends of these arms were hands, opening and closing into fists. Gershwin tossed a rock at the bumper. The left arm shot out, with the sound of a whip cracking, and crushed the stone to dust.

Gershwin sat cross-legged on the asphalt. Passing cars blew his hair from its careful part. He stared. The hands flexed.

He stood up carefully, brushing the dirt off of his khakis. He inched his way back around the car. The hands did not follow him. He opened his passenger door and pulled his phone out of the center console.

His first few attempts to call failed. He held his phone up to the sky. The third time he got through. A voice on the other end, impatient. When he talked he could hear his voice echoing back at him. He could hear himself breaking up. The voice on the other end asked him, "What do you mean your car broke down?"

The call dropped. Gershwin put the phone back in the center console. He reached into the backseat and held the gift wrapped box in his lap. Shook the thing. Played with the bow. Buying this was the first thing he did after he got the call. After getting black-out drunk. After buying a new cell phone. After crying in his car. After holding the phone to his forehead, groaning at the floor, then breaking it against the wall. After hearing the voice on the other end, all business, telling him that his son had been in an accident. IED. Roadside bomb. He was alive, the voice had said. But his legs were lost in the blast.

Gershwin had only said one word into the phone, repeating what he heard, "lost," almost like it was a question. He had felt the next few days piling up in front of him. He'd hung up and cried

He held the box to his chest with one hand and covered his face with the other.

The car started quietly. He pulled onto the highway and called the number again. Told his ex-wife that he got the car running again. Shouldn't be long.

She said, "He lands in an hour."

And Gershwin said, "I'm hurrying. I'm on my way."

He felt the weight of the trip. He saw the blacktop in front of him. He saw silhouettes in the passing cars. He saw wheels. He had strange premonitions: the plane touching down, seeing his son for the first time in a year, waving, full uniform. Gershwin couldn't picture how the boy would look below the waist.

His nerves were all shot to hell. He passed a clean blue sedan and he looked over and saw the driver: a young woman with big sunglasses and full lips, staring down into the blue glow of a cell phone. The sedan lazed over the median, close, until Gershwin could have rolled down his window and touched it. He slammed on his brakes and honked his horn. From behind the sedan, he saw the driver swerve the car back into its proper lane, look in her rear view mirror, and flip him the bird.

The car hummed.

Righteous indignation fomented in Gershwin's stomach. He ground his teeth until his jaw cracked. He sped up until he was next to the sedan and turned his head. The woman's face was down, again, staring at her cell phone. Thumbs in motion like insect legs. She laughed at something on the screen and flicked a lock of hair behind her ear.

The blood rushed to Gershwin's head and the car began to shake with such force that the gift box bounced from the passenger seat and onto the floor. The white arms growing from his bumper expanded. He could see them in his rear-view mirror, the muscled arms flexing and callused fingers groping. Gershwin gripped the steering wheel till he could feel the pressure of his blood in his veins, and the vengeful white arms got big as hot air balloons. The hands blocked out the sun.

They clasped together, as though in prayer.

The woman kept her head down, unaware of the great shadow looming over her. She glanced at the road once, when she veered too far and rolled over the rumble strip on the side of the highway.

The white arms hung above her like a guillotine, like a giant thought bubble stretching from the bumper of Gershwin's tiny car.

The woman put her cell phone in the cubby under her radio and placed both hands on the wheel. She looked up, took her sunglasses off, and screamed.

The climax shuddered through him, the giant hands coming down on the crown of the car, folding it upwards, the hood and the trunk kissing in the sky. Giddy vindication clogged his sinuses. He watched the destruction in the rearview, the crumpled scrap heap turning end over end into a ditch, as the hands began to shrink, deflating like a balloon along with his rage, until he couldn't see them anymore, until they were gone.

Gershwin took a deep breath and combed his hair into a part with his fingers. The anger inside of him was temporary, something that would pass. Vague embarrassment, a promise never to do it again, that would be all it would leave in its wake.

He checked himself in the mirror and leaned over the gearshift. He picked the gift box from where it had fallen on the floor and placed it on the passenger seat. He patted it like a child and turned on the radio. Old white men shouted at each other. Old white men hated foreigners. Old white men hated gays. Old white men hated the youth, couldn't stand them, couldn't stand their lack of respect, their selfishness, their ignorance. They couldn't stand those kids who text and drive.

Gershwin turned up the radio. He nodded his head.

The car hummed.

Subversion is, in many ways, the soul of Bizarro. But in this case, unbridled political subversion rears its inescapably ugly head, with an assist from good ol' Nature herself.

Jeremy claims, "This story qualifies as Bizarro via the Cronenberg Character Study (Plus Nastiness) Clause." I agree, in that it's that kind of dangerous.

It also throws me back to the underground comics of the 60s and 70s—I'm thinking brilliant Last Gasp Eco-Funnies like Skull and Slow Death—in that it both embraces the Green hippie case and shames its absurdities all to hell, in stunningly honest tail-swallowing fashion.

Cathedral Mother
by Jeremy Robert Johnson

One *little piggy dies and the whole crew goes soft.*

Amelia saw things for the way they were. No bullshit. You had to see straight or The Machine would grind you down, leave you blind, fat, and confused. *Stare at the hypnotic box. Have another slice of pizza. There's cheese in the crust now!*

She brushed aside a chest-high sword fern, feeling the cool beads of a just-passed rain soaking into her fingerless climbing gloves. The redwood forest was thicker here, and the gray dusk light barely penetrated the canopy. Amelia tried to force herself calm, taking in a deep breath through her nose, picking up the lemony tang of the forest floor, a hint of salt air from the Pacific, and the rich undercurrent of moist rot that fed the grand trees and untold species. She imagined herself in the time of the Yurok tribes, when man had a fearful respect for this land, before he formed the false God of the dollar and built McMansions of ravenous worship.

She found no calm. All thoughts trailed into spite. All long inhales exited as huffed sighs of disgust.

Goddamn fucking humans. The worst.

When she joined The Assemblage she had felt like they understood. They *got it*. They could see The Machine for what it was—a vast system established solely to allow the human virus to replicate and consume at any cost. And The Assemblage had formed to restore balance.

She'd only met one other member of The Assemblage, as a precursor to her redwoods mission. Their group thrived in the anonymity of a subnet supposedly facilitated by a sixteen-year-old kid who'd been vying for membership in a hacker group with a classy name—World Wide Stab. So instead of having a batch of finks and fuck-ups gather in somebody's musty patchouli patch living room with an inevitable COINTELPRO-variant mole, The Assemblage existed only as a loosely organized forum of people who understood The Machine and challenged each other to disassemble it in as many ways as possible.

Minks were liberated from a farm in northern Oregon, their pricey cages devastated after the exodus. Two Humvee dealerships in Washington got hit, one with well-placed Molotovs, the other with thousands of highly adhesive bumper stickers reading "NAMBLA Member and Proud of It!" Chimps were saved from HIV testing at a bio-tech development firm outside of San Diego, and subnet photos showed them being returned home to a preserve in Africa (where, Amelia guessed, their lack of survival skills probably got them torched as "bush meat" shortly thereafter). Every Wal-Mart in New Jersey arrived to glue-filled locks on the exact same morning.

Not everything The Assemblage pulled was to Amelia's liking, but overall they seemed to be one of the only groups out there worth a damn.

That was until the Oregon tree spiking incident shook them up.

She'd been shocked too, initially, when she opened the forum thread. The title read, "97% of Oregon Old Growth Gone—Don't Fuck With Our Last 3%." Two quick clicks on the title and she was staring at a grainy, zoomed-in digital photo: a logger's face turned meatloaf, head nearly bisected, left eye loose of its orbit. Text beneath that: No more warning signs for spikes! Let's *really* put Earth first! Feed the worms another tree killer!

The Assemblage, for all its rhetoric and snarky misanthropy, was not prepared for murder. Buddhist members cried bad karma. Pacifists quoted Gandhi. Anarchist kids sweated clean through their black bandanas, wondering if eco-terrorist association charges would make Mom and Dad kill the college funds. Membership dwindled in anticipation of Fed heat.

Amelia, however, was applauding. The Oregon spikers got it right. Now The Machine was short a cog, and she knew any logger working that territory had a new thought in their head: *Is this worth dying for?*

She was inspired. She knew that acres of redwoods south of her home in Eureka were about to be offered up as a smorgasbord to a conglomerate of corporate interests, one of the final parting gifts from King George's administration.

She had hiked those territories since her childhood, and even now she trekked there with her son Henry. The trees there were giants, vast even among redwoods, some topping thirty five stories tall, with trunks over twenty feet around. To her they were great and ancient things, representatives from better times.

To grow for thousands of years only to be destroyed for the "cubic feet" needed to house more goddamned MOB's (Morbidly Obese Breeders, Assemblage code for the common-folk) . . . Amelia couldn't stomach the idea.

She planned. There were only a few months until the virgin forest was to be royally fucked by bulldozers and cat-tracks and chainsaws and cranes.

Despite being consumed with finding a way to stop The Machine from gaining penetration, she tried to stay balanced.

Nights were for plotting—surveying and copping gear and staying tuned to those few voices on The Assemblage that still raged and let her know she wasn't alone.

Days were for Henry—homeschooling and hiking and lessons in doing no harm. Late summer heat let them swim in a pond near their property, sometimes until dusk brought out flurries of gnats and insect-chasing bats. These were the sorts of things she pointed out to Henry, to remind him that he needn't be jealous of the TV shows his friends talked about.

Not that she let Henry see those friends too often. Their life was very contained, and she couldn't risk outside influence turning her son into another one of . . . them.

She never intended to become a Breeder,

and had a hard time accepting the extra pressure she was creating for the taxed environment. But she reminded herself that she had not had Henry for selfish reasons. She'd been young, and confused, and had made the mistake of being seduced by a gangly hippie boy named Grant, who was drifting through town with a few hundred other friends on their way to a Rainbow Family gathering.

She was pulled away from the boredom of her grocery store stock clerk gig in Eureka, and spent over a year wandering the US with the Family, dropping acid and shitting in woodland troughs, shoplifting steaks and air duster (for cooking and huffing, respectively). Free love gave her a nice case of genital warts and a disappearing period.

Grant, lover that he was, offered to sell off his Phish bootlegs to pay for an abortion, but by the time she'd really put the pieces together she was already in second trimester, and the kicks in her belly had her feeling like this kid was closer to alive than not. She killed the LSD and nitrous habits and smoked a lot of weed and ate buckets of trail mix and waited for the Rainbow Family train to circumnavigate back toward Eureka.

The train didn't quite chug fast enough and she ended up having Henry on the outskirts of a field in eastern Oregon, near the Blue Mountains. A girl named Hester, who claimed to be a midwife, shouted at Amelia to breathe. Then, once she confirmed Amelia was indeed breathing, she shared what she must have thought was comforting wisdom.

"The Armillaria mushroom that grows near here is the biggest living thing on Earth. It's underground. It's like three miles wide."

Then she wandered off into the distance, perhaps to find this giant mushroom, leaving Amelia alone to have the most primal experience of her life.

She felt abandoned for a moment, cursing Grant for his carelessness, herself for being seduced by the irresponsibility dressed as freedom that brought her to this Third World state. But loneliness was swiftly crushed by a series of contractions and a sense of animal purpose. Then everything was waves of pain, and a sudden release, and the sound of tiny lungs taking first air. Amelia collapsed with her boy, loneliness long forgotten.

She was cradling Henry in her arms when a dirt-bag named Armando wandered by and offered to help. He also, she later realized, wouldn't stop looking at her crotch. Still, he had a Leatherman, and in cutting her umbilical, was the closest thing Henry had to an obstetrician.

With her infant son in her arms she'd found it easy to beg enough change to get a Greyhound Bus ride back to glorious Eureka.

Since then she'd done her best to raise Henry outside of an ever-sickening American culture. If she had to be a Breeder, she'd make damn sure that her contribution to the next generation gave back to the Earth in some way. Since she couldn't trust Henry to the goddamned Rockefeller Worker Training Camp they called Public School she'd had to reconnect with her parents and beg enough of a stipend to support her and the kid.

It meant her parents got to visit Henry on occasion, but she was sure to let him know that these were Bad People. Industrialists. Plastic makers. Part of the Problem. They were piggies.

Still, they kept her and Henry in the food and clothes business, and Amelia took a secret joy in spending their money on the various laptops and servers that maintained her connection to the subnet and The Assemblage.

And lately she'd been spending their cash on climbing gear. It had taken her a precious couple of weeks to come up with her plan, but if she pulled it off she'd be able to protect the forest *and* keep it from being tied to her or her new associate.

She'd drafted "Cristoff" from another subnet board called Green Defense, where he'd developed a reputation for being too extreme. His avatar was a picture of Charles Whitman with the word HERO embossed at the bottom.

They vetted each other via subnet friends. "Cristoff" agreed to drive up from San Francisco so they could get to work. Real names, they agreed, would never be exchanged.

Posing as husband and wife—Mr. and Mrs. Heartwood, har har har—they hooked up with a local arborist named Denny who gave lessons in recreational tree climbing down by the Humboldt Redwoods State Park.

Henry was allowed to spend a week with his friend Toby (whose family she found the least disgusting).

She and Cristoff were quick learners. They picked up "crack-jamming" on day one, which allowed them to free climb a redwood's thick, gnarled bark by pinning hands and feet into the crevices. Day two taught them how to use mechanical Jumar ascenders, rope, and a tree climbing saddle to get much higher. This was called "jugging," a term which Cristoff found amusing.

"I'll tell my buddies I spent all week crack-jamming and jugging with a new lady friend."

Who was this guy? *And* he had friends? That was concerning.

Still, he could climb, and was willing to help her with the delicate work they needed to do up in the unprotected redwoods.

At night she wore a head-lamp in her tent and read up on great trees: Forest canopies held half of the living species in nature. The top of the tree was the crown, which could be its own ecosystem, several feet across, filled with canopy soil up to a meter deep, hosting hundreds of ferns, barbed salmonberry canes, even fruit bearing huckleberry bushes. These crowns were miracles of fractal reiteration, with some sprouting hundreds of exacting smaller versions of the main tree, all of them reaching for the sun. The redwoods were one of the last homes for legions of un-named prehistoric lichen and some canopies even inexplicably harbored worms and soil-mites previously thought to be extinct.

She was particularly happy to read that both HIV and Ebola were postulated to have come from human interaction with canopy dwelling primates and bats. These trees were already fighting back. It gave her mission a sense of camaraderie. She would work with these noble giants as an advance warning system. *Don't fuck with our last 3%.*

Amelia and Cristoff spent the last part of their lessons learning a technique for which they'd paid extra. Skywalking was a way of manipulating multiple ropes and knots in the upper canopy, allowing you to float from branch to branch without applying too much weight. Properly done you could even move from crown to crown.

They *had to* be able to do this, as the crowns they'd be leaving would be far too treacherous to allow return. They were going to create a logger's nightmare up there.

That was the plan—To spend a week camped among the canopies, working to saw dozens of branches just short of the snapping point. The loggers and climbers call these hanging branches "widow-makers" and with good reason. Falling from stories above they could reach terminal velocity and they typically tore loose an armada of forest shrapnel on their way down. One turn-of-the-century account of a widow-maker dispatch simply read, "Wilson was ruined. Pieces were found five feet high in surrounding trees. The rest of him was already buried beneath the branch. Most could not be retrieved for proper interment."

How many loggers would be splattered by her old growth nukes before they asked the crucial question?

Is this worth dying for?

That *was* the plan, at least until Cristoff decided to get in a fight with gravity.

There are different types of branches on a redwood. The higher branches can be thick as most regular trees and are rooted deeply into the trunk. The lower branches are far narrower. Between handfuls of strawberry granola Denny had told them these lesser branches were called epicormics, or "dog's hair" for slang. They were easily shed and not to be trusted.

Cristoff was getting comfortable in the trees, pleased with his progress. Denny told them not to be surprised if this felt strangely natural, since all other primates were at least partially arboreal.

Cristoff's inner monkey had him gassed up and proud after a few strong ascents. Cristoff's inner monkey started feeling an imaginary kinship with the tree. The kind of false trust that let him think a batch of epicormics would hold as well as a single trunk-rooted branch.

He was sixty feet up, ten feet past the climber's "redline" cutoff for survivable falls. He ignored Denny's request that he rope a higher branch. The last thing he said through the walkie talkie was, "I've got this."

The redwood, clearly disagreeing, decided to shed some weight.

The sounds were as follows: a sharp crack as the branches separated, a shocked yell accompanied by a terrible whooshing sound as gravity got serious, and at last a chimerical whoomp-crunch as Cristoff created the first and only Cristoff Crater at Humboldt Redwoods State Park.

Technically, per Denny's lessons, he was supposed to yell "Headache" if any object was falling, even himself. His neglect would be forgiven the moment Denny and Amelia approached his body.

Cristoff was breathing, but the crimson gurgles at each exhale screamed hemorrhage, and compound fractures at the femur and clavicle had happened so fast that the bone still jutted white and proud with little blood to emphasize how shattered the man was.

Still in shock, Denny informed Cristoff that he shouldn't move.

As far as Amelia could see, this was a non-issue. Whoever this Cristoff was, she had a hard time imagining he'd ever move again.

Denny held out hope, lucking into a cell phone signal and getting Air Life dispatched.

Amelia tried to get Cristoff's eyes to focus on hers, but his were glazed and the left had gone bright red. She could hear a helicopter in the distance.

She prayed for telepathy. She stared at the broken man and thought, "Don't you say a motherfucking word."

With that, she turned and walked to her rental Chrysler. Denny's eyes stayed fixed on the injured man as "Mrs. Heartwood" gunned the car out of the park, leaving an odd impression, some cheap camping gear, and the crushed shell of a man she hoped would die, and fast.

Weak men were shaping Amelia's

world. First Grant left her with an STD and a kid. Then the spiked logger's greed and split skull became the catalyst that weakened the resolve of The Assemblage. Now the man she knew as "Cristoff" turned snitch.

It wasn't intentional, but the bastard (real name: Richard Eggleston) had managed to make it to the hospital, and the opiate mix they pumped into him for pain management left him delirious. His night nurse picked up enough chatter about "tree bombs" to feel comfortable playing Dutiful Citizen and calling the Feds.

The Feds got to his computer gear. The subnet that hosted The Assemblage was fluid enough that they were able to block Fed access and re-route themselves, but speculation about what might have been on Eggleston's hard drive had a variety of already-freaked underground groups on full black helicopter alarm.

Worse still, The Assemblage had gone even more limp-dicked. Even staunch hard-liners she'd once trusted were calling the glimmers of her plan that had gone public "monstrous and irresponsible."

She put her stress in the wrong places, snapping at Henry for minor transgressions like leaving his crayons out. She was forgetting to eat.

Then a new voice joined The Assemblage— Mycoblastus Sanguinarius. *Black bloody heart.* She looked it up and discovered the namesake was a tiny lichen that revealed a single dot of blood-like fluid when ruptured.

He signed his posts as Myco. She assumed the member was a "he" since the writing had a masculine terseness, but there was no way to be sure.

Myco posted an open letter to anyone who might have been involved in the aborted "redwoods plan." He begged them to contact him privately, saying that he might have a way to help them reach their goal without shedding any blood.

He had to be a mole, right?

She ignored Myco and tried to come up with her own new plan. Random spiking? Fire-bombing bulldozers?

The stress amped her self-loathing. *You say you hate humans. Well, what do you think you are, bitch? What do you think Henry is? Chain yourself to a tree and starve out. Pull the media into this. How much explosive could you strap to your body? To Henry?*

These were not safe thoughts. She pushed them away. She tried to stay focused on a real option. The loggers would gain access soon.

She sent a non-committal message to Myco. *What's your plan?*

Two days later Myco sent a response, and it felt legit. He *was* government, and he was upfront about it. He held a position of some influence, and if he had the right information he could get it in front of someone who might have the power to halt the government's release of the property.

The problem was that the property was in a weird transitory status, off limits for government-permitted climbs even for the research sector. He needed someone who knew the area to engage in a "ninja climb" and acquire a number of biological samples. Depending on what was found, the rarity of the species and its "viability for government use," he might be able to prevent the destruction of those groves.

But who was this guy? This was a classic COINTELPRO move. He wrote like a professor, which could place him with DARPA or one of its extensions. Could just be an FBI grunt telling her what she wanted to hear. And would it be any better if the property was retained "for government use?"

Or was this some old hippie college teacher trying to regain his idealism after trading it for a BMW in the '80s? Maybe his son was in the California legislature? Maybe his nephew was the goddamned President?

Who knew? But she trusted this subnet, and if he promised they'd never have to meet then she felt there was enough safety in the agreement. There's no way he'd be able to guess which trees she'd climb. The groves were too dense, the old timber too wide.

He assured her that all he needed were the samples, and she could leave them in a place of her choosing, as long as it was temperate and hidden. Then she just had to forward the location via GPS coordinates.

It would be a shame to waste her climbing lessons. And she'd been dreaming of these trees, somehow still standing proud for another thousand years, after all the little piggies had destroyed each other. In her dreams the skyscrapers fell and the redwoods swayed in the moonlight, returned to their post atop the world.

She responded to Myco—Please check Assemblage regularly. Location of samples to follow.

After sending was confirmed she crawled into bed with Henry and spooned him, despite a few sleepy grumbles. She pulled the blankets tight around the two of them and kissed the back of his head.

I'll protect us, Henry, from these humans.

A**ll** of her gear was black, from boots to ropes to pack. Even her Treeboat, which would allow her to sleep in the tree hammock-style if needed, was damn near invisible at night.

Dusk had passed now, and her anger was shifting to nerves as she tried to recall climbing techniques. She moved quietly. The yielding forest floor, rich with decomposed needles and ferns, absorbed much of her noise. Where moonlight broke through the thickening canopy it revealed large clusters of redwood sorrel, the heart-shaped leaves still glowing emerald green in the slight illumination. It was beautiful.

I will save this place.

She picked a full moon night, thinking it would give her better natural light once she cleared the canopy and reached the crown. Until that point she'd have to stay to the shadows.

Myco told her that the older the tree was, the more likely it was to be biologically diverse. She searched for the base of a redwood that looked about three cars across, and briefly shone her headlamp to check the coloration of the bark. The "newer" trees, only a few hundred years old, would have reddish brown bark while the eldest would have shifted to a stony gray.

Her tree finally presented itself, after forty minutes of hiking deeper into the grove. Light had simply ceased to find a home. To her right she saw the outline of the blockage, a tree thick as a blue whale reaching up to heights she couldn't perceive.

She ran her hands across the bark, imagining herself at the foot of some planet-traversing colossus who was standing still to allow her up for a visit.

She used a pair of night vision-equipped Zeiss binoculars to scan the base for a solid climbing branch on which to start. The best option was about one hundred and forty feet up, though several epicormics presented below that. She thought of "Cristoff's" ruptured eye and wrong-angled bone shards and immediately canceled any thought of risking the lower points.

The best solution was to shoot a weighted fishing line over the good branch, then use that line to pull a rope back up and over. It was a patience game, and she set herself to it, unpacking a crossbow with a pre-threaded dull-tipped arrow.

Four tries and she found purchase. After that it seemed easy to rig up the rope and lock in her climbing saddle and Jumar ascenders.

She began her climb beyond the world of the humans, praying that the tree's nightlife would yield something Myco needed. She stopped at each major branch and briefly flipped on her headlamp, extracting a plastic container with a micro-fiber lid as instructed by her mysterious correspondent. The lids allowed oxygen in, but nothing, even water, would find its way out.

At mid-height she managed to pry loose a tent spider entrenched in a bark pocket. Its eyes gleamed purple in her headlamp.

She scored fragments of lichens, some shaped like leaves of lettuce, others like tiny clothespins, and still others that looked like green beard hairs.

Just before breaking into the crown she spotted an inverted blackened chamber about three feet wide, the damage from some fire that likely burned before the birth of Christ. Tucked just inside the fire cave she found a blind salamander, its damp wet skin speckled with orange dots. She grabbed a chunk of moist canopy soil to include in its container so that it might survive the voyage.

The salamander wiggled in her fingers. She stared at it, wondering how the hell it got up here.

Speaking of which, how did I get up here?

Strung between two branches, hundreds of feet above the Earth, staring at some tree lizard. Way out of cell phone range and one mistake away from instant death. So far from home, from Henry.

Aside from the thought of her son, she was filled with exhilaration rather than fear. This was a world so few had ever seen. And she was going to save it from her terrible species.

Emboldened, she pushed upward to the crown. The moon was there to greet her, blindingly bright and so close she could touch it.

Amelia was confused during her descent. Happy, ecstatic really, but confused. She felt as if her time in the crown was a dream. Beautiful to be sure, but . . . those things couldn't have happened, right?

She'd been gathering more samples—a variety of berries, more lichen than she could count, even a bright white worm she spotted nosing out of the canopy soil. But then she'd . . . what?

Shimmers of light. *She'd found the trunk pool.* Dead center in the crown, the main trunk had collapsed inward and hollowed out, allowing water to collect there.

She'd reached in with a plastic sample container and immediately felt a sting in her exposed fingers. Was it the cold? But seconds later her hand filled with warmth. It spread up her arms and unfurled in her chest. She'd closed the sample container and tucked it into her pack.

Then she remembered feeling an overwhelming sense of joy, and safety. Thoughts of rotten Grant or all the pigs snorting around down on Earth turned to sand and were blown away. A dumb grin slid across her face and the moon blurred through her tears—a white puddle surrounded by oil.

But did she really unhitch her tree saddle and carabiners? Did she really let her body drop into the trunk pool, and float there, picturing herself as a tiny red hummingbird sitting in the palm of a kind and loving God.

It seemed insane. But when she reached up to feel her hair, it was still sopping wet.

"I had a moment of rapture," she thought. And she didn't care if it was real or not.

She descended carefully, methodically, and placed her cargo in a safe place before the sun cracked the horizon.

After cleaning up and communicating her drop spot to Myco, she drove to Toby's parents' house to pick up Henry. She still hadn't slept, but she couldn't wait to see her son. There was something so lovely about him. She smiled at the thought of him and her chest ached in his absence. She sped across Eureka, keeping an eye out for the erratic driving of the tweakers that inhabited early morning commutes like this. Not that she hated the tweakers. Everyone had their problems.

Jesus, what?

Amelia had been clean of the poison of drugs for a long time now, but she could swear she was being washed over by waves of euphoria. She wrote it off to sleep deprivation and adrenaline.

But when she got to Toby's she found that instead of honking and waiting for Henry to come running out, she practically jumped out of her car and ran to the front door.

Shit. I'll have to talk to the parents.

I love the parents.

Oh, God.

Thankfully only Henry emerged from the front door. Amelia saw him recoil as she crouched down to sweep him up. What a boy . . .

"Momma, you smell funny."

"Well, kiddo, you smell, too. You smell *great*. God, I just love you SO MUCH!"

She kissed him full on the lips, a big wet smacker that she was sure would have embarrassed him if Toby were watching. Oh well, she'd slap one on adorable little Toby too.

She set Henry down. He looked up at her, his brow furrowed. "You okay, momma?"

"Yes, honey, I'm better than ever. You want to go get some pancakes?"

With that he nodded "Yes" and took off running for the car. He *never* got pancakes. High fructose corn syrup was a poison, one of the favorites of The Machine.

But it felt so right to make him happy. She wanted to hold him close and kiss him all over his little face.

He was already buckled when she got in the car. He was rubbing his sleeve back and forth on his lips.

"It tingles, momma."

"Bad tingles, like burning?"

"No, like peppermint. It's kind of nice, I guess."

"Are you sure?"

"Yup. It's really nice, actually. Really nice."

She and Henry were barely eating anymore. They felt constantly tired, though they found they were happy just cuddling and drinking water. Lots of water, to the point where Henry would laugh at the sloshing sounds when either of them moved around.

Their temperatures ran hot, but never to the point where she started thinking Emergency Room.

Amelia did worry when the sores appeared on Henry's chest and arms. They reminded her of the splotches on the tweakers that tried to shoplift at the grocery store she'd worked for. Her boss had told her that was caused by battery acid in the meth.

She applied A & D Ointment to Henry's sores and got a cool washcloth for his forehead. That seemed to give him more energy. He asked her to tell the story again, about climbing the great tree and meeting the strange creatures and swimming in the sky pool and saving the woods.

He loved the story. He loved her and told her so, over and over again.

He was dead when she woke.

She could tell right away. She was so hot—sweating under the blankets—that his body was like ice against her chest.

And something was very wrong. Because his chest was not expanding, but his belly was. His abdomen was thrumming like it was filled with boiling water. Worse, while her animal instinct got her away from his body, she found herself back in front of the sink, refilling her favorite glass with tap water. Good God she was thirsty.

And happy.

Happy? Fucking Christ—Henry is dead. Something is moving in his belly.

They'd both been crying for days now, but they were tears of overwhelming joy, at their luck that they might be alive and filled with so much love.

Amelia wanted true tears. Part of her brain was screaming, begging to collapse to the floor, to crawl back to Henry and wail.

What was happening?

For days now, their lives were only bed/ water /love. They'd heard helicopters roaring overhead last night, and it was a wonderful sound. That man should fly was so amazing.

No. Henry is dead. Nothing is amazing. Figure out what's going on.

Drink some water.

No.

Go to bed.

No.

She hadn't turned on her computer since sending her last email to Myco. *What a beautiful name. What a great man!* Amelia wanted to scrape all this love out of her skull, but it came at her in insistent waves.

Myco had responded: Your woods are saved. Your collection efforts provided us with not just one, but *two* viable interests. Rest assured that this grove will be protected for some time to come, though public access will be greatly reduced. However, the trees will be saved, and I would like to let you know, in the confidence afforded to Assemblage members of course, that one of the lichen you provided us may hold the key to boosting white blood cell counts in patients with severe immune deficiencies. The other sample of interest was a microscopic parasite found in the water sample you provided. We expected protozoa but actually discovered a never-before-seen type of copepod, a tiny shrimp-like creature. We can't tell whether it has been self-sustaining in the tree for thousands of years, or if it was just recently dropped there by a wet-winged osprey, but we do know that it possesses an ovipositor for egg delivery and that the eggs have this miraculous viral coating that likely induces confusion in the host. It's similar to how a parasitic wasp breeds, but it is *so streamlined*. You've done our group a great service and we believe that this little management tool may help us to control invasive fish species off of Florida and elsewhere. Congratulations!

She deleted the message.

Henry's body was twitching under the blankets.

Drink more water.

Get in bed. Love your son.

Protect him.

She refused the voice. It was a virus. Myco's precious streamlined management tool had killed her son, and it would kill her too. And for the first time in her life, she could embrace her death.

But not Henry's. Poor Henry.

Before she died she was going to send a message to some of the piggies. Somehow they'd led her to this terrible place. *All these humans . . .*

Amelia cleaned herself, ignoring

the shifting in her own belly and the "love" that whipsawed around her brain.

She dried and put on her only perfume and spotted a few sores blooming on her skin. Nothing some foundation couldn't cover up.

She slid on a short skirt and an old black t-shirt. It fit perfectly—the last few days' fast had done right by her looks.

No underwear. None needed.

She would walk to the outskirts of the grove, where she guessed gun-sure soldiers and salivating business men were already setting up perimeter in anticipation of harvesting what she'd found.

There was an old redwood stump there which had refused to die. It was fifteen feet across and rimmed on all sides by new redwood trunks growing from its edges. The locals called these "fairy circles" and a few romantic visiting botanists had termed them "cathedrals."

She would claim this cathedral as her own and would invite every last man to join her.

She licked her lips in anticipation. She was already wet. Her upper thighs tingled. Like peppermint. It *was* really nice.

Humanity needed a management tool. And she would give it to them.

With love.

In marketing, your brand is everything; and it's as true for Bizarro as it is for McDonalds. We are all, for better and worse, distinguished by our special sauce.

And so we close with this Happy Meal of mind-blowing virtuosity, by yet another genius who didn't even know she was Bizarro till I read her the ingredients on the back of her psychic packaging.

Violet says, "This story was dictated to me by my subconscious in an unbroken, complete epic dream. It was a gift among gifts, and I knew when I awoke I'd be a fool to throw it away."

And I would be a fool indeed if I didn't share this phenomenal story with you.

Rough Trade Marks the Spot
by Violet Glaze

Maybe she was Hmong and maybe she was Filipino, but on Monday morning the flat-faced immigrant hired for the morning shift at Scrum-Chee Burger fell back in a faith healer swoon. Eyes rolling in her head like a doll, half moons of white bobbing behind Venus flytrap lashes. Boils appeared on the inside of her wrists. The blisters broke and something creamy and pink came bubbling out.

I was dreaming thick and comatose dreams when the phone rang.

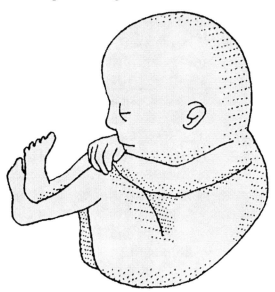

"Dress but don't shower," crackles my lieutenant's voice.

"Who it is?" murmurs my wife as I slide out of bed. The amber light behind the Venetian blinds juliennes the landscape of her pregnant body into slices. Like cultivation furrows on rolling farmland.

"Just a look-see," I whisper, laying a hand on her belly. She groans and shifts away.

I chop out a line of pulverized wake-me on the bathroom porcelain and try not to snort too loudly. Halfway out the door the cold shower inside my skull turns on full blast. The drive is easy. The overcast sky is the color of blueberries and milk.

Henderson greets me at the Scrum-Chee burger door. "It's not so bad," he says, lifting the crime scene tape. Last year Henderson told me a mummified play group stuffed into three suitcases and a diaper bag was "not so bad." I can do without his brand of optimism.

I flash my badge. Forensics workers scuttle aside.

"One month to go, Daddy-o?" Henderson grins. He smashes a pale wad of gum between his tobacco-yellow teeth. It appears and disappears like a bald baby mouse in the razor pegs of a push mower.

"Three weeks," I say. Pregnancy's measured in weeks by those who live it, months by everyone else. I've absorbed my wife's terminology.

My wife.

She used to be a contortionist in a traveling circus. Boneless, I tell you. Soles of the feet on the top of her head, crack of her ass resting like a pillow on the small of her neck. My god, I was one lucky fucker the first year we were together. Then she got tired of me sniffing after her rubber spine all the time. Sorry, cowboy, it happens to all married men.

I'm still happy, though.

Henderson let out a low whistle. "They say you wanna stand behind them. That way you don't see the little monkey come out. Makes it easier to get it up again, you know?"

When we met, she thought she was infertile. No worries. More fun when you don't have to tip the piano player, if you know what I mean. But a year ago it really got to her. That magic thirty years and five, it makes women take to their beds and stare at the ceiling as they feel their eggs go sour. Then *boom*, like that, pregnant. She's been on bedrest for the last two months. No backbends, no splits, no headsits. She doesn't complain. I always knew she was a trouper.

I'm going to be a daddy.

Henderson leans over the insensate woman sprawled on the herringbone brick of the burger joint floor. "Her name's Guadalupe Maron. Guatemalan national." Henderson squints. "What's that crap on her face?"

"Special sauce." The forensics guy looks up from his plastic baggies and motions towards her body with two fingers, like a flight attendant pointing out the exits. "Leaking from multiple exits, natural and inflicted. Tear ducts, wrists, a gash in her side." He pushes his glasses up onto his nose. "Didya ever have the Scrumburger? That's the sauce they use on it."

"Someone put it on her?"

"Naw. It's in her blood. It *is* her blood, actually."

"Corporate stigmata," I mutter. A lowest level employee manifesting the sins of the parent corporation in her body. Try that transubstantiation on for size.

"Wasn't there a case like this in Old Town a while back?" I ask. Someone takes a picture. The flash glints off the oily sauce.

"Yeah, at the Sterback's Java Hut," says the forensics guy. "Hot espresso running in every vein. Poor fucker got boiled from the inside out. Lotta blood in the liver. Lotta blood in the brain."

Henderson turns to me. "So there's this guy who runs a hotel with an infinite number of rooms," he says. "One guest in each room. No vacancy. But an infinite number of people show up at the front desk one night. And they all want a room. What do you do?"

"Make all the guests move down one." I say, dabbing at the corner of the woman's eye. "Old guests get the even numbered rooms, new guests get the odds." I smear the sauce between my fingertips. Feels like warm mayonnaise. I didn't taste it to be sure.

Henderson thinks he can stump me with kindergarten brainteasers. Fat chance. I'm a registered logician, PhL first degree. I get called out when crimes defy logic. Not "I ate my baby" logic, but real cracks in the universe's laws. Puzzles like that hotel question seem paradoxical but actually cling to the rules like a Cub Scout in church. A hotel with an infinite number of rooms can never be full, no matter how many guests show up. Infinity plus infinity is still, always, infinity. Making them take the odd and even numbers is just a classy touch.

"Last night, everything in the universe doubled in size," I say to Henderson. "Prove me wrong?"

Henderson takes a moment to think about it. "Get a ruler from somewhere else," he concluded.

"Mm." I say. "Good one."

Puzzles like why this poor woman had to die for Scrum-Chee Burger's sins don't have an easy answer. There's been more of these kinds of stumpers lately. The world's getting slippery. That's the thing about living in the last days of a logical universe. Everything could be carrion and concrete dust already and you'd never be able to deduce a thing.

Henderson unwraps a fresh stick of gum. "Any big ideas, Mister Peepers?"

I shake my head. "The only place things get weird like this is on the quantum level. But never this kinky."

The world gets dull all of a sudden.

"Where's the john?" I hear myself ask.

Two minutes later there's a fresh surge of powdered aleratamol in the dense capillaries of each of my nostrils. I gotta cut this shit out before the baby's born.

When the baby's born.

I want to take him to the ocean.

I loved the ocean when I was a kid.

"Hey." Fists pound on the door. "Come on out. We've got trouble."

Suits. Maybe high-up Scrum-Chee, maybe not. 1960s G-men black coat and tie, discreet stripes of red and gold ribbon above the lapel. I can't read corporate rank but I figure the guy with two stripes is the boss of the guy with only one.

"We'll take it from here," Two Stripes says, in the alpha dog baritone of a nature film narrator.

"Can't." Henderson chaws his gum. Baby mouse, baby mouse. "Crime scene."

"You're on private property," says Two Stripes. One Stripe nods. "And Saint Guadalupe was our employee."

"Pretty quick to canonize her there." I step in. "You're certain this isn't a kinky homicide? Might look pretty stupid if you start handing out prayer cards with the Happy Lunches before we determine this isn't the work of the Condiment Killer."

"Miracles are not a matter for sick jokery," said Two Stripes. "But that's what I expect from a logician." He said it like *child pornographer*.

I take another look at Two Stripes' insignia. "Where did you say you were from again?"

He didn't answer. I didn't expect him to.

They carried Guadalupe Maron out on a cross-shaped tray. Same nubbly orange plastic they give you to balance your burger. Same paper placemat cut to fit. Two Stripes and One Stripe clutched the tray lip like pallbearers and bore her into the van. The van door had a symbol. A cross with two bars. Double dagger. The kind they use for footnotes in ad copy, to make sure you read the trademark notice at the bottom.

"They're not Scrum-Chee," I hiss to Henderson.

Henderson shakes his head. "Vatican™ if I ever saw it."

I sighed. Vatican™ meant no information was going to flow towards this case, and no information was going to flow away from it, either. Vatican™ was the wall of calcified plaque on the artery of my job. I should have stayed in bed.

Henderson looks down. "What's wrong with your hand?"

I look down. The tips of my fingers, the parts that press together when you pinch, are covered in a bubbling salmon-colored rash. I shake my fingers

involuntarily but you can't flick off what's already a part of you.

"Jesus, wash that off!" says the forensics guy. He tosses me a bar of carbolic soap. I make a beeline to the bathroom.

Scrub, scrub, scrub.

When I'm done scrubbing I call my wife to check in. I tell her not to eat Scrum-Chee Burgers. I can hear how her voice changes as she wrinkles her nose in disgust.

"I never eat that stuff," she says.

Good.

Back at the office I start tracking down everyone Guadalupe Maron knew in this country. No surprises. She was a devout Catholic. She worked three jobs, all at different burger places. Scrum-Chee, Delightaburger, Char Hut. Maybe she was singled out for stigmata because of her devotion, both to church and all-beef patties. By whom, I haven't a clue.

At nine there's another one. Char Hut, Center City. Fat widow trudging her cottage cheese hips through the narrow aisle between fry machine and shakes suddenly can't finish the lunch rush. "Her hips got wider and wider," the teenage witness tells me. His scrawny shoulders shudder inside his polyester uniform. The polyester doesn't shudder with him. "Her tits swole up like balloons."

I make a note of it.

"Test for antibiotics and bovine agricultural hormones," I tell the forensics guy as he steps

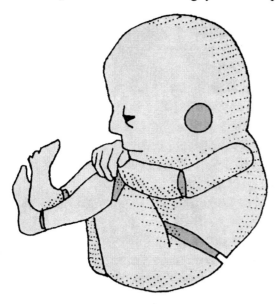

gingerly around the puddles of colostrum still pooling on the floor from the gigantic corpse's still-leaking breasts.

"You think it's the same?" crackles Henderson over the phone.

"I think someone's getting back at Big Fast Food through their employees," I say. "Payback for all the sludge their factory farms dump in the ocean."

The ocean.

When I was a kid the ocean was the color of an overcast sky. The color of blueberries in milk. Now it's dark as cola.

I want there to be something left for my son. I want him to stand on the shore and watch the tides come in, relentless. One soaring roar after another, each wave a domino stroke from currents deep inside a vast and limitless sea. I know now that it's not vast and limitless. But once upon a time, when I was little and cute and my nostrils weren't singed with wake-up, that sea was like the infinite hotel with an infinite number of rooms.

If you want more room, just move one over.

"What's your plan?" says Henderson.

"People are predictable," I say. "They go to the same places and do the same things. I'll notice the logic in their actions that they don't."

The Char Hut case name was Debra Devinge. I interview her co-workers. Insect scat at the bottom of the corporate terrarium. They don't have anything useful to say. So I go back to the office and busy myself with the illusion of work. Follow up this phone call, so-and-so wants to see you, stroll for another corrosive cup of coffee that doesn't even dent the cry for wake-up hammering in my veins.

"Hey, hijinks," says Henderson, slamming his hands down on my desk. "A momma and a baby are walking on a beach. Suddenly a crocodile comes up and grabs the baby in its teeth. The momma screams, but the crocodile won't let go. Croc says 'Will I eat your baby?' Tell me the right answer and I'll give him back."

I cut to the chase."There's no answer. It's a paradox. If the mother says 'You *will* eat my baby,' and she's right, the crocodile has to give the baby back because she's telling the truth. If she's wrong, the crocodile won't give the baby back. He'll eat it. Which makes her right, and he has to give the baby back anyway."

"Wrong." Henderson's eyes glinted like the tips of two spears. "Crocodiles don't talk, pal. That baby's dead."

The calls kept coming in. A fry cook at Taco Queen. Skin boiling over with golden blisters, every sebaceous gland shooting a pimple geyser of hot hydrogenated oil. A cashier at Hoagie King, the cellulite under her wrinkly thighs clustering like sprouted cauliflower and swarming under her flesh, strangling her major organs in a waxy white blossom of fat. They were bleeding ketchup from the eyeballs and drooling barbeque sauce from swollen gums and disgorging milkshake from mouth to asshole, like a creamy case of cholera. Not much in sales today.

"Meeting," yells the chief. "Conference room. Now." I shuffle in. Henderson's already dimmed the lights. I take a seat close to the screen.

"Here's how it stacks up," said Henderson as his shadow points at the first row of vignetted heads on the family tree. "Aunt Jemima, Quaker Oats guy, Betty Crocker. 'Undocumented,' as the Vatican™ likes to call them. They won't admit some ad executive cooked them up, so they just say the details of their earthly life have yet to be discovered. Next slide."

I take paper and pencil from my pocket and draw up a quick logic grid puzzle. Aunt Jemima lives next to the man who likes pancakes. The Quaker Oats guy is not in the red house. Betty Crocker smokes Trebuchets, menthol. Just something to keep my mind off the one-note symphony pleading in my brain for more wake-up.

"Next row—Duncan Hines, Chef Boyardee, Sara Lee. These chuckleheads have made the big leap from jabbering around with the rest of us to corporate immortality. They were all real people, born and died, and now they're up in the stars with Tony The Tiger and whatnot. That's Vatican™'s story and they're sticking to it."

"Now we've got this new wave of unexplained sudden deaths," Henderson continues. The slide changes. I didn't realize we've already logged 29 fatalities this morning. 29 martyrs passing through the Golden Arches of Paradise. "The Vatican™ wants their sticky little fingers in the pile. Our question is why?"

"Talk to their guy," someone pipes up in the back.

"No access. They're suddenly very hush-hush."

"What a surprise," I grumble. I put my pencil back in another pocket and brush my fingers against a glassine envelope of wake-up. Back in a jiff.

In the men's room I discover only crumbs at the bottom but that doesn't stop me from licking it clean like a cupcake wrapper. I gotta cut this out. Three more weeks and then I'm cold turkey.

Back in the meeting room I lift my hand to itch my nose and the chief thinks I'm volunteering. Next thing I know I'm in the back of a cruiser with Tomkins on my way to visit a spokesperson.

"You go for this mumbo jumbo?" Tomkins sneers as he lights a cigarillo.

"Nothing mumbo about it," I say. "Legally, a corporation is no different than a human being. It needs to consume, to grow, to excrete, to reproduce. But it has no body. When it needs to speak, it has to borrow another set of lungs and lips and tongue. That's where the spokespeople come in."

The cruiser glides up to the curb of the spokesperson district. I make sure to avoid the gutter.

There's spokespeople in storefronts stacked on storefronts, like a wall of aquariums in a pet store. Like Amsterdam whores in anchorman clothes. I pick one that looks friendly.

"Good morning! My name is Sandra." She's a little old to still be a spokesperson so maybe she'll try harder for less money. "How can I help you gentlemen today?"

"We want to speak to the Vatican™," I say. "Barring that, something from Char Hut, or the parent company for Scrum-Chee."

"I'll see what I can do," she trills, and turns a dial on something at her ear. Something in her head clicks off and her eyes go blank as a doll's for a few smiling seconds. She clicks back on. "Vatican™ is not responding to inquiries today. I can try the other places you mentioned, or I can see if there's someone else who can patch me into the Vatican™."

"Give the Vatican™ another try," I say. "We've got time."

"Mmm-hmm." She brushes her fingers past the device on her ear. No, it's not on her ear. It's replaced her ears, both of them. Probably goes straight through her skull like a toilet paper roll. Eyes like a doll again. Wait.

"You have reached the Vatican™," the voice booms out of her.

I get gooseflesh. I flash my badge.

"We're investigating several unexplained phenomena at downtown fast food outlets," I say. "Your agents seems to take a lot of interest in what's happening among the corporation's lowest level employees lately."

"We take an interest in many avenues of business," says Sandra in that reptile-calm voice. The picture on the computer behind her is starting to bend and moire. Electromagnets can do that. I suddenly get uneasy about what's whizzing in the air around us. I wonder how many more years Sandra can do this before the tumors start crawling through her brain like spindly fireworks.

"Yesterday two of your agents carried one of our crime scenes away on a cafeteria tray," I say. "Now there's a pandemic of fast food virulence and you're giving each minimum wage McJobber a pharoah's send-off. Why the pomp and circumstance? You waging some kind of pan-corporate war against the Burgermeisters?"

"Vatican™ is a majority shareholder among Scrum-Chee, among others. We do not wage war upon ourselves." Her voice drops an octave. I feel low frequencies massaging anti-stress hormones out of my amygdala. "But we are excellent in power and in judgment. We don't afflict unnecessary pain. This is the key to our respected position on the global market. Besides – those people were lucky to have a job."

"Bullshit," I spat. "Any time you want to start making sense, feel free."

"I see you're not at liberty to discuss this," the voice purrs. "Please call between normal business hours if you need further assistance. Have a nice day." Sandra clicks her tongue and the connection terminates.

"Thanks, Sandra," I say, swiping my card through the "OFFERINGS" terminal at the front of her table. "Come on, Tomkins, let's get out of here."

"Thanks for visiting," Sandra chirps. A leisurely bead of blood is dripping from her nose almost all the way into her Vaselined smile. Being an oracle enacts a price on your body. She doesn't brush the drip from her face. Must be the same temperature as her skin.

Back in the cruiser we pass a sub shop on 18th and Market. "Wait here," I say, tumbling out of the car. "I love the onion rings."

I step up to the grease-stained window at the far back and exchange paper money for five glassines from the scowling cashier.

"Where's your onion rings?' Tomkins asks as I step back into the car.

"They fry them in baby oil," I sneer. "Can you believe that?"

"Gotta die of something," he sighs, and peels out.

Back at the office I manage to pace the wake-up over the next few hours. A little game I like to play with myself, to prove I'm still a recreational user. One at 1 o'clock, one at 2:10, one at 3:20, one at 4:10 because I can't wait, and one at 4:50 as a reward for waiting the other times.

Calls are still coming in at closing time. Employees are filling up with deforested wood pulp, slaughterhouse lagoon water, E. coli infestations. Bumpy rashes suddenly break the skin, revealing the bloody points of plastic straws and coffee stirrers. Reverse crucifixion, porcupine style. I call my wife to let her know the boss wants me to stay.

"You have to come home," she says, her voice tight. "I think I'm in early labor."

I feel my guts turn to mint.

"Are you sure?" I quaver. "Did you call the doctor?"

"I did," she said. "I'm scared. Come home."

When I fly through the door my wife is laying in bed.

"False alarm," she says. "Little fish is wriggling."

I put my hand on her belly. Something hiccups under my palm, like a neighbor tapping on the wall of the next apartment over.

"Strong," I say.

"Sure," she says. "Like his dad." She shifts under the covers, the sound of cotton on cotton like the roar of the ocean.

"We haven't been to the ocean in a while," I say.

"That's because I hate it there. All that sand."

"You don't have to stay on the sand. You go into the water." I slide my hand down the crest of her hip. "Washes it right off."

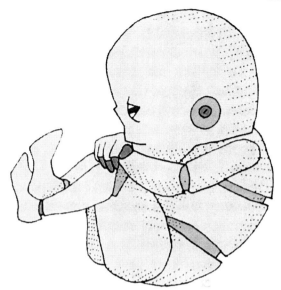

"And sticks right to you again on the way out." She sighs. "But he's your son, so he'll probably have a good time."

"You sure about that?" I bury my face in the crook of her neck. She smells like yeast and sweat and clean at the same time. Good.

She turns and looks at me. "I'm sure it's yours," she said, with a gravity I didn't really care for.

"I meant the good time," I say.

The phone goes off at my belt.

"Paranoia is one of the first signs of aleratamol intoxication," says the smooth spokesperson voice through the little tinny speaker. "Fears of persecution and conspiracy, especially those close to you. A burning, oozing rash, especially on the extremities."

I look at the raw chancre on my fingertip.

"Who are you?" I spit into the phone.

"The woman laying next to you is not your wife," the voice continues. "Lift up the covers and you'll see the mechanism that allows you to believe you feel her fetus under the palm of your hand."

I freeze.

"What is it, honey?" she says.

I yank back the covers. They didn't spend money on latex skin from the breastbone up.

I rip the white polymer off the belly container and find the robot inside. It doesn't look like a baby. It's just a mechanism. Balls on clockwork sticks, moving like little fists.

"You look like you've seen a ghost, honey." The android mouths its script, not realizing I've torn it open, sternum to legless groin.

I shove it aside and bury its face under pillows so I don't have to look at it.

"Where is my wife?" I scream into the phone.

"Memory loss is a common side effect of long term alertamol use," says the voice. "I will now give you directions. You will retain them only for the duration of your journey, and then you will forget, irrevocably."

"I'll forget jack *shit*!" I scream, and suddenly I'm in the warehouse, big and dark. Catwalk grates beneath my feet. A gigantic pool of luminescent water glowing beneath me.

I stare down. My wife is in the pool. She floats on her back and kicks like a sleepwalker. Her eyes are fixed. Her pregnant belly is real.

I lunge at the catwalk rail and two monstrous homunculi rush at me and grab my forearms in their gigantic chubby hands. Skin black as racehorse flesh, red baboon lips jutting beneath goggling incandescent eyes. They crush me between their hard toddler bellies and I feel the air cough out of my lungs. I stare up at their giant infantile craniums bobbing and nodding on weak necks, like wilting parade balloons.

"Do you seeing that thing swimming round and round?" says one through its too-fat lips. My face is smashed against its navel. I look down and see the red tutu slung under its waist. Black letters printed on the crumpled crinoline. GOLD DUST.

"Mmm," the other blubbers. "Maybe we can reaching in and make it drown."

"Get your fucking paws off of me," I try to snarl, but my ribs won't expand. I feel stale air going acid in my lungs.

Help.

"Goldie, Dustie—" A suave and continental voice insinuates between their humid flesh and into my ears. "Let him go."

They drop me to the catwalk. I shovel oxygen into my lungs as quickly as I can, and look up.

A well-dressed man descends the catwalk, nimble as Fred Astaire. Top hat, bow tie. Big grin. Face in shadow.

He steps into the light and the shadows stick to his face.

"Darkie," I gasp. "Darkie Toothpaste."

"That's Darlie," he nods. "Darlie with an L," He raises his sharp chiaroscuro fingers to the brim of his hat. "The North American market's a touch sensitive these days. But you can call me Mr. Hei Ren. 'Mister Black Man'. That's what the Chinese still call me." He smiles. I squint involuntarily from the brilliance of his grin.

I've never seen a trademark in person before. I don't like it.

Mr. Hei Ren brushes dust from his cuffs. "Aunt Jemima, Uncle Ben, Rastus on the Cream of Wheat box – for some reason the public doesn't object to them. But The Gold Dust Twins and I can't go out in the light of day anymore. So we work behind the scenes. Black ops. Excuse the pun."

"Give me back my wife," I threaten.

"Can't," says Mr. Hei Ren, unruffled. "She's giving birth."

"What—?" I say, and stare over the catwalk edge just in time to see something fat and slick slide out from between her thighs in a burst of underwater blood.

I gasp, and tear at the railing.

Can I jump?

I can't jump.

My wife. My son.

My son.

I lunge at the grate again and the Gold Dust Twins pin me to the floor.

"He's going to drown!" I shriek into the sawtooth grate.

"He's fine," says Mr. Hei Ren." You'd do best to leave him in the water."

I see between the catwalk slits. My son is circling the swirling water, sleek as a dolphin. One lap, two laps. He's pink. He's healthy. He's not dying. He's swimming. He's breathing.

Little fish.

She begins to disintegrate. Shreds of skin peeling like the aftermath of a bad sunburn. The water clouds with skin and fat, like soup stock. The white bones rise to the surface. Then the first layer of synthetic collagen starts to dissolve.

Not bones. Links of snaky scored metal. They twine sinuously in the water.

A contortionist.

Boneless, I tell you.

The metal snakes undulate like seaweed and sink to the bottom. They spiral in a rosette around the drain.

"No!" I scream.

"No need for hysterics," Mr. Hei Ren says. "She outlived her usefulness." He pulls pencil and paper out of his breast pocket. "Shall I draw you a grid?" He presses the paper against my back and I feel him draw five neat rows, five neat columns. He checks off each row as he explains.

"First off, you were right about the quantum level. It's rare for things in the real world to get quite so . . . *queer* without involving some kind of quantum trickery. So bravo to you, PhL, first degree. But you're so suspicious," he continues. "You think everyone's trying to do the corporations in. When in fact . . ." He chuckled, a warm movie star laugh that melted even my fear. "We're too big to worry about anyone taking us down."

"Who's us?" I sputter into the floor.

Mr. Hei Ren gave me a condescending look. "Corporations, Vatican™ . . . You know." He looks at me, his high contrast face twisting in amusement. "Let's have a little fun, logician. Why do fast food hamburgers taste so good?" he asked.

"Because they're full of crap," I spit. "And chances are, they'll kill you."

Chance.

It dawns on me.

"Particles." I look at Mr. Hei Ren. "You put quantum particles in the meat."

"Bravo," says Mr. Hei Ren. "Flash frozen dog tripe from Mexico City does not taste good ground into a burger. Neither do human gristle, or surgical scraps, or medical waste. But put enough probability warping particles in the mix . . ." He shrugs. "Special sauce covers the rest."

"But you lost control," I snarl. "Feed enough people, handle enough warped food day in and day out, and reality starts fraying. And your lowest level employees, the people who come in the most contact with the warped particles, start paying for your corporation's sins."

"See, we knew you'd figure it out. Matter of fact, we knew because of our own probability warping technology predicted it. So we started planning our revenge ahead of time." He motions to the pool where my son still floats. He's only a blur of sleek, amphibian pink.

I want to hold him.

"Do you seeing that thing swimming round and round?" says Goldie.

"Till human voices wake us and we drown." says Dustie.

"We built the android that became your wife," says Mr. Hei Ren. "We exploited her inhuman flexibility because we know what you like, you cheeky devil. We made her a contortionist in a traveling circus and we sent you the tickets. We engineered your marriage."

"That's bullshit. My wife loved me."

"Yes, it's true. We didn't count on her developing human emotions. Or her desire to truly father your child. Maybe the hormone load of all that spunk you pumped into her was clouding her brain. All we know is, she stopped coming here to make her weekly, uh, deposit." He wags his finger, tsk-tsk. "Cloning takes raw material. You were just giving it away."

"Bullshit," I sneer. "She's been on bedrest for the past two months."

"She's not on bedrest, pal. She ran out the door when she saw we were coming this afternoon. Had to stick a needle in her neck to bring her here."

I want to kill. With superhuman effort I shrug my way out of the Gold Dust

Twins' grasp. Both of them go over the railing and into the soup of my wife. They dissolve into black shreds like torn balloons. Thank god, they don't hit my son.

I grab Mr. Hei Ren by the neck and squeeze. "Give me back my son," I hiss.

Mr. Hei Ren presses his cufflink. The pool's drain opens. It's a big drain . . .

My son flows out, down the drain like a belly-up goldfish.

My son.

"Don't worry, you've got more," says Mr. Hei Ren breezily. " He was only the newest. We've farmed plenty of you. Adults, not children. Perfect clones. They're on the scent. They'll probably kill you in a week."

"They'll never find me," I say, and squeeze harder.

"People are predictable," chokes Mr. Hei Ren, that big smile not leaving his face as his voice constricts. "You know that. Your clones will go where you go and do what you do. Except once they see each other, they'll be overcome with an inexplicable urge to kill, a feeling of sheer violent rage unlike anything you've ever experienced. Except probably now."

He still smiled at me as I choked harder. His larynx crumpled under my purple thumbs but he kept talking.

"So go on," he croaked. His black and white face was turning bloated and gray. "Be free. Enjoy the things you like. Go to the restaurants and bars and movies you enjoy. Sooner than you think, you'll meet someone who likes the exact same things. And you'll have lots of catching up to do. Everyone always wants to meet their soulmate," he gasped. "Lucky . . . lucky . . . youuuu."

I drop his lifeless body and look around. The clones are coming for me, very soon. They are making coffee in my house, ordering onion rings and wake-up at seedy takeout windows, tolerating Henderson's riddles and counting the days to fatherhood. They will see each other and kill each other. Then only the strongest one will be left.

But I have a plan.

I will leave all my regular haunts behind. I will head to the ocean. When I was a kid I loved it there, more than I've ever loved anything in my adult life. More than logic puzzles. More than onion rings. More than wake-up. More than my wife.

But not more than my son.

If my son is truly made from my DNA, he will be there too.

And I will find him first.

About the Contributors

Michael A. Arnzen is the author of the flash fiction collection *100 Jolts: Shockingly Short Stories* (Raw Dog Screaming Press) and the Bizarro novella, *Licker* (Novello Publishing). He has four Bram Stoker Awards and an International Horror Guild Award on his trophy shelf, right next to his dismembered hand collection.

Amelia Beamer's debut novel *The Loving Dead*, with zombies and a Zeppelin, has been praised by the likes of Peter Straub, Christopher Moore, and John Skipp. Read the first four chapters for free at ameliabeamer.com.

Nicole Cushing may be a new bizarro author, but that hasn't stopped her work from appearing in some highly respected venues for weird storytelling. Eraserhead Press debuts Nicole's first book, the dark satire *How To Eat Fried Furries*, at Bizarro Con 2010. Her short fiction appears in the John Skipp mass market anthology *Werewolves And Shapeshifters: Encounters With The Beast Within* and the long-awaited Cemetery Dance Richard Laymon tribute anthology *In Laymon's Terms.* Nicole counts Thomas Ligotti, Phillip K. Dick, and H.P. Lovecraft among her influences, and often blogs about them on her website, www.nicolecushing.com.

Robert Devereaux lives in Colorado, intending eventually, foolish man, to save the world through his fiction. He's the author of *Slaughterhouse High*, *Santa Steps Out*, *Santa Claus Conquers the Homophobes*, *Deadweight*, *A Flight of Storks and Angels*, and other instances of fabulation.

Kevin L. Donihe, perhaps the world's oldest living wombat, resides in the hills of Tennessee. He has published six books via Eraserhead Press. His short fiction and poetry has appeared in The Mammoth Book of Legal Thrillers, ChiZine, The Cafe Irreal, Dark Discoveries, Poe's Progeny, Electric Velocipede, Not One of Us, Dreams and Nightmares, Bust Down the Door and Eat All the Chickens, and many other venues. In the past, he edited the Bare Bone anthology series for Raw Dog Screaming Press, a story from which was reprinted in The Mammoth Book of Best New Horror 13. Visit him online at www.facebook.com/kevin.l.donihe

Violet Glaze started her writing career as a film critic and arts journalist for various print and on-line publications in the US (including *Baltimore Magazine, City Paper, Popmatters.com* and *Urbanite*) and the UK (*The Little Black Book: Movies*). A parallel shadow career as a slash fictionista led her to penning erotic novels *Hotel Butterfly* (2009) and *Will Success*

Spoil Pace Hammond? (slated for 2011) and the short story collection *I Am Genghis Cum* (2010). She lives in Philadelphia.

Cody Goodfellow has written three novels (*Radiant Dawn*, *Ravenous Dusk* and *Perfect Union*) and a story collection (*Silent Weapons For Quiet Wars*) solo, and three books (*Jake's Wake*, *The Day Before* and *Spore*) with John Skipp. His "short" fiction has appeared in Cemetery Dance, Black Static and Dark Discoveries, as well as the anthologies *The Bleeding Edge*, *Monstrous*, *Mighty Unclean* and *Cthulhurotica*.

Marcy Italiano is the author of *Pain Machine*, *Spirits And Death In Niagara* and *Katrina And The Frenchman: A Journal From The Street*. She lives in Waterloo, Ontario with her husband and two year old twin boys, working on websites at night and yet, still can't stop writing.

Jeremy Robert Johnson is the Bizarro author of the cult hit *Angel Dust Apocalypse*, the Stoker Nominated novel *Siren Promised* (w/ Alan M. Clark), and the end-of-the-world freak-out *Extinction Journals*. His fiction has been acclaimed by Fight Club author Chuck Palahniuk and has appeared internationally in numerous anthologies and magazines. In 2008 he worked with The Mars Volta to tell the story behind their Grammy Winning album *The Bedlam in Goliath*. In 2010 he spoke about weirdness and metaphor as a survival tool at the Fractal 10 conference in Medellin, Colombia (where fellow speakers included DJ Spooky, an MIT bio-engineer, and a doctor who explained the neurological aspirations of a sponge). Jeremy runs Bizarro imprint Swallowdown Press and is working on a host of new books.

Marc Levinthal has been involved with both "The Music Business" (having written the hit single "Three Little Pigs" while in the band Green Jello) and the "Motion Picture Industry" (having co-written the score for the cult classic *Valley Girl*). He's also published numerous short stories and novellas, plus the Bizarro fantasy novel *The Emerald Burrito of Oz* (with Skipp). He and his wife Rebecca presently spend much of their time caring for two chimpanzees disguised as small children. (The chimpanzees, not Marc and Rebecca. That would be wrong.)

D. F. Lewis received the British Fantasy Society Karl Edward Wagner Award in 1998. *Weirdmonger* (Prime 2003) collected some of his stories. A novella, *Weirdtongue,* is published this month by The InkerMen Press. And he is currently seeking a home for his novel, *Nemonymous Night*. He published the *Nemonymous* anthologies from 2001 to 2010.

Livia Llewellyn is a writer of horror, dark fantasy and erotica, whose fiction has appeared in ChiZine, Subterranean, Sybil's Garage, PseudoPod, Apex Magazine, Postscripts, and several erotica and horror anthologies. Her first collection of stories is coming out in 2011 from Lethe Press.

J. David Osborne lives in Norman, OK. His first novel, *By The Time We Leave Here, We'll Be Friends* will be out soon from Swallowdown Press.'

Cameron Pierce lives in Portland, OR. He has served time as a paperboy, a taxidermist's assistant, a shellfish farmer, an extra in a Gus Van Sant film, and a college dropout. Now he just writes books. His latest are *Lost in Cat Brain Land* and *The Pickled Apocalypse of Pancake Island*.

John Skipp is a *New York Times* bestselling writer, editor, zombie splatterpunk champion, and notorious horror bigshot. His books include *The Light at the End, The Cleanup, The Scream, Deadlines, The Bridge, Animals, Fright Night, Book of the Dead*, and *Still Dead* (with Craig Spector); *The Emerald Burrito of Oz* (with Marc Levinthal); *Jake's Wake, The Day Before*, and *Spore* (with Cody Goodfellow); *Opposite Sex* (as Gina McQueen); *Conscience, Stupography*, and *The Long Last Call* (solo); and, as solo editor, *Mondo Zombie, Zombies: Encounters with the Hungry Dead*, and *Werewolves and Shapeshifters: Encounters With the Beast Within*. He lives with family/friends, both human and otherwise, on a hill overlooking the glistening spires of downtown Los Angeles.

Melanie Skipp is a self-proclaimed "professional bohemian freek baby." The spawn of a recovering porn star and an acclaimed horror novelist, she has had one of the most exciting and horrifying childhoods one could fathom. Currently living in California with the afore-mentioned father, Melanie enjoys reading childrens books and horror novels, playing video games, getting tattooed and attempting to outwit her two insane cats Lord Phinneus Hallow, and Poluchik Dimitri Chevok Horus. She also enjoys blowing bubbles. Mmm, bubbles.

Leslianne Wilder says, "About me? I'm a native of Austin, Texas (largest urban colony of bats in the world). My two mothers released a documentary about the Texas obscenity laws and sex toys called *The Dildo Diaries*. I'm currently studying to be an EMT and I just returned from Egypt where I went on a bedouin camel trek through the Sinai Peninsula."

D. Harlan Wilson's latest books include *They Had Goat Heads* (fiction collection), *Peckinpah: An Ultraviolent Romance* (novel), and *Technologized Desire: Selfhood & the Body in Postcapitalist Science Fiction* (literary theory). In November, Wilson will begin traveling around the US, Canada and Europe on The Zero Degree of Meaning Tour to promote *Codename Prague*, the second installment in his scikungfi trilogy. Learn more at www.dharlanwilson.com.

Introduce yourselves to the bizarro genre and all of its authors with the Bizarro Starter Kit series. Each volume features short novels and short stories by ten of the leading bizarro authors, designed to give you a perfect sampling of the genre.

"The Bizarro Starter Kit" (Orange)

Featuring D. Harlan Wilson, Carlton Mellick III, Jeremy Robert Johnson, Kevin L Donihe, Gina Ranalli, Andre Duza, Vincent W. Sakowski, Steve Beard, John Edward Lawson, and Bruce Taylor.

"The Bizarro Starter Kit" (Blue)

Featuring Ray Fracalossy, Jeremy C. Shipp, Jordan Krall, Mykle Hansen, Andersen Prunty, Eckhard Gerdes, Bradley Sands, Steve Aylett, Christian TeBordo, and Tony Rauch.

"The Bizarro Starter Kit" (Purple)

Featuring Russell Edson, Athena Villaverde, David Agranoff, Matthew Revert, Andrew Goldfarb, Jeff Burk, Garrett Cook, Kris Saknussemm, Cody Goodfellow, Cameron Pierce

"Warrior Wolf Women of the Wasteland" Carlton Mellick III - They call themselves the Warriors, their enemies call them the Bitches. They are a gang of man-eating, motorcycle-riding, war-hungry werewolf women, and they are the rulers of the wasteland. A century after the fall of civilization, only one city remains standing. It is a self-contained utopian society protected by a three-hundred-foot-high steel wall. They are content and happy, blindly following the rules of the fascist fast food corporation that acts as their government. But when Daniel Togg, a four-armed bootlegger from the dark side of town, is cast out of the walled city, he soon learns why the state of the outside world has been kept secret. The wasteland is a chaotic battleground filled with giant wolves, mutant men, and an army of furry biker women who are slowly transforming into animals.

"The Emerald Burrito of Oz" John Skipp and Marc Levinthal - ZOMBIE MUNCH-KINS! TURD-FLINGING FLATHEADS! EVIL CORPORATE CONSPIRACIES! DELI-CIOUS MEXICAN FOOD! OZ IS REAL! Magic is real! The gate is really in Kansas! And America is finally allowing Earth tourists to visit this weird-ass, mysterious land. But when Gene of Los Angeles heads off for summer vacation in the Emerald City, little does he know that a war is brewing...a war that could destroy both worlds! This loving Bizarro tribute to the great L. Frank Baum is an action-packed, whimsically ultraviolent adventure, featuring your favorite Oz characters as you've never seen 'em before. Let super-hot warrior sweetheart Aurora Quixote Jones take you on a guided tour of surrealist laffs, joy, and mayhem, with more severed heads than Apocalypse Now and more fun than a barrel of piss-drunk winged monkeys!

"Super Giant Monster Time" Jeff Burk - Aliens are invading the Earth and their ray guns turn people into violent punk rockers. At the same time, the city is being overtaken by giant monsters tougher than Godzilla and Mothra combined. You can choose to be a lone scientist trapped in a secret government lab on a remote island swarming with monstrous killer insects, a badass punk rock chick with a green mohawk caught in a bar room brawl as the city goes up in flames around her, or a desk jockey forced to endure tedious office duties while his building is being attacked by a gargantuan centipede with claws the size of sports utility vehicles. Which character will you become?

"Ass Goblins of Auschwitz" Cameron Pierce - In a land where black snow falls in the shape of swastikas, there exists a nightmarish prison camp known as Auschwitz. It is run by a fascist, flatulent race of aliens called the Ass Goblins, who travel in apple-shaped spaceships to abduct children from the neighboring world of Kidland. Prisoners 999 and 1001 are conjoined twin brothers forced to endure the sadistic tortures of these ass-shaped monsters. To survive, they must eat kid skin and work all day constructing bicycles and sex dolls out of dead children. While the Ass Goblins become drunk on cider made from fermented children, the twins plot their escape. They must overcome toilet toads, cockrats, and ass dolls. Forget everything you know about Auschwitz... you're about to be Shit Slaughtered.

"Perfect Union" Cody Goodfellow - When Drew married Laura, he also married into the Kowalski family. But on a trip with his twin brothers-in-law into the backwoods of northern California to find their abusive, estranged mother, buried secrets will be revealed, threatening his fragile marriage and his sanity. Mom has joined a new family: Leviathan-- a utopian colony that has taken the communist ideal to radical biological extremes, using the mutagenic honey from genetically tweaked bees to make ideal workers and flawless warriors. But the once-human hive is divided by a strike and brutal internecine war, and its tyrannical Chairman is eagerly recruiting scabs. With the Kowalski twins taking opposing sides in the colony's bitter feud, Drew is forced into a world where nothing is taboo and survival is the only law, where he must negotiate between the insane collective mind and the savage refugees, even as the battling forces of the commune work to reshape him into a tool to complete their . . .

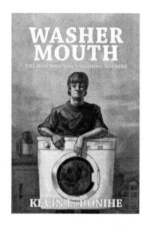

"Washer Mouth" Kevin L. Donihe - Roy is a washing machine messiah. Recently turned human, he must pave the way for the coming of the washer-men. Unfortunately, Roy is not a very good messiah. More obsessed with the daytime Soap Opera Sands of Eternity, Roy deviates from his mission in order to follow his dream of acting in a scene with its beautiful leading lady, before she is retired from the show. But Roy soon discovers that the rise to stardom isn't a simple task, especially for man whose mouth is an out-of-control washing machine. A menagerie of freaks, bukkake hair treatments, sexually deranged divas, super powered superstars, snuff films, gloop lunches, and a murderous washing machine man known only as "The Dark Washer" all await Roy on his quest through the bowels of the day-time drama industry. It's The Little Mermaid meets O'Lucky Man, filtered through Futurama.

"Super Fetus" Adam Pepper - Try to abort him, and this fetus will kick your ass! He's a fetus growing in the womb of a whiny white trash whore of a mother. His problem: she wants to have him aborted. But what this bitch doesn't know is that she isn't pregnant with some mild-mannered developing human form. Heck no. This is Super Fetus. He has an attitude and he is determined to be born, whether she likes it or not. Doing push-ups in the womb day and night, until he becomes amazingly buff, this little fetus is prepared to fight off the onslaught of vacuums, tongs, coat hangers, and scalpels. Once that sonofabitch doctor comes for him . . . he'll be ready. Too tough to be aborted, Super Fetus fights back!

"Fistful of Feet" Jordan Krall - A bizarro tribute to Spaghetti westerns, H.P. Lovecraft, and foot fetish enthusiasts. Screwhorse, Nevada is legendary for its violent and unusual pleasures, but when a mysterious gunslinger drags a wooden donkey into the desert town, the stage is set for a bloodbath unlike anything the west has ever seen. His name is Calamaro, and he's from New Jersey. Featuring Cthulhu-worshipping Indians, a woman with four feet, a Giallo-esque serial killer, a crazed gunman who is obsessed with sucking on candy, Syphilis-ridden mutants, ass juice, burping pistols, sexually transmitted tattoos, and a house devoted to the freakiest fetishes, Jordan Krall's Fistful of Feet is the weirdest western ever written.

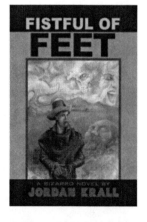

"Shatnerquake" Jeff Burk - William Shatner? William Shatner. WILLIAM SHATNER!!! It's the first ShatnerCon with William Shatner as the guest of honor! But after a failed terrorist attack by Campbellians, a crazy terrorist cult that worships Bruce Campbell, all of the characters ever played by William Shatner are suddenly sucked into our world. Their mission: hunt down and destroy the real William Shatner. Featuring: Captain Kirk, TJ Hooker, Denny Crane, Rescue 911 Shatner, Singer Shatner, Shakespearean Shatner, Twilight Zone Shatner, Cartoon Kirk, Esperanto Shatner, Priceline Shatner, SNL Shatner, and - of course - William Shatner! But these Shatner-clones are about to learn a hard lesson...that the real William Shatner doesn't take crap from anybody. Not even himself. It's Shatnertastic!

"Slaughterhouse High" Robert Devereaux - It's prom night in the Demented States of America. A place where schools are built with secret passageways, rebellious teens get zippers installed in their mouths and genitals, and once a year, on that special night, one couple is slaughtered and the bits of their bodies are kept as souvenirs. But something's gone terribly wrong at Corundum High, where the secret killer is claiming a far higher body count than usual . . . Slaughterhouse High is Robert Devereaux's slicing satire of sex, death, and public education.

"Pickled Apocalypse of Pancake Island" Cameron Pierce - A demented fairy tale about a pickle, a pancake, and the apocalypse. It is Gaston Glew's sixteenth Sad Day - the sixteenth anniversary of the saddest day of his life: his day of birth - and his parents have just committed suicide. Fed up with the sadness of Pickled Planet, Gaston Glew builds a rocket ship and blasts off into outer space, hoping to escape his briny fate. Meanwhile, on Pancake Island, Fanny Fod, the most beautiful pancake girl in the world, nurses a secret sadness as she guards the origin of all happiness: the mysterious Cuddlywumpus. When Gaston's rocket ship crash-lands in the sea of maple syrup that surrounds Pancake Island, nothing will ever be the same for him, or for Fanny Fod.

"The Kobold Wizard's Dildo of Enlightenment +2" Carlton Mellick III - ARE YOU READY TO PLAY SOME DUNGEONS AND FUCKING DRAGONS? The Kobold Wizard's Dildo of Enlightenment +2 is an absurd comedy about a group of adventurers (elf, halfling, bard, dwarf, assassin, thief) going through an existential crisis after having discovered that they are really just pre-rolled characters living inside of a classic AD&D role playing game. While exploring the ruins of Tardis Keep, these 6 characters must deal with their inept Dungeon Master's retarded imagination and resist their horny teenaged players' commands to have sex with everything in sight. Featuring: punk rock elf chicks, death metal orcs, porn-addicted beholders, a goblin/halfling love affair, a gnoll orgy, and a magical dildo that holds the secrets of the universe.

"Help! A Bear is Eating Me!" Mykle Hansen -Trapped in a remote Alaskan forest, pinned under his own SUV, gnawed upon by nature's finest predators, Marv Pushkin --Corporate Warrior, Positive Thinker, Esquire subscriber -- waits impatiently for an ambulance and explains in detail the many reasons why this unfolding tragedy is everyone's fault but his own.

"Silent Weapons for Quiet Wars" Cody Goodfellow - In the brutal zero-sum game of the new future, every meal is a murder, and every act of love is a declaration of genocidal war. To survive it, you will have to make alliances with the sleeping demons in your blood; learn to wear new names and faces, and shed your soul; feed your inner child to the machine, before it eats you alive; build and defend your own heaven; and become one of the sacred, secret tools with which nature reinvents itself. To win this game, you will have to change into everything that you are not. To play you need only open this book.

"The Vegan Revolution . . . With Zombies" David Agranoff - Presenting Stress Free Food! Animal suffering is a thing of the past. Hipsters can now enjoy bacon without guilt. Thanks to a new miracle drug the cute little pig no longer feels a thing as she is led to the slaughter. The only problem? Once the drug enters the food supply anyone who eats it is infected. From fast food burgers to free-range organic eggs, eating animal products turns people into shambling brain-dead zombies - not even vegetarians are safe! In Portland, Oregon, vegans, freegans, abolitionists, hardliners and raw fooders have holed up in Food Fight, one of the country's premier vegan grocery stores at the vegan mini-mall. There they must prepare for their final battle to take back the city from the hordes of roaming undead. Will vegans filet the flesh-eaters or will they become zombie chow? When there's no more meat in hell, the vegans will walk the earth.

"Rock and Roll Reform School Zombies" Bryan Smith - Sex, Death, and Heavy Metal! If you're a teenage metal head The Southern Illinois Music Reeducation Center is not the place you want to go. The center specializes in "de-metaling" – a treatment to cure teens of their metal loving, devil worshiping ways. A program that subjects its prisoners to sexual abuse, torture, and brain-washing. But tonight things get much worse. Tonight the flesh-eating zombies come . . . *Rock and Roll Reform School Zombies* is Bryan Smith's tribute to "Return of the Living Dead" and "The Decline of Western Civilization Part 2: the Metal Years."

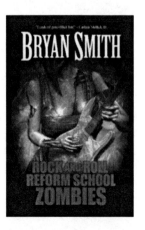

"Angel Dust Apocalypse" Jeremy Robert Johnson - You can survive a nuclear blast. All you need is some luck, and maybe a customized business suit coated in cockroaches. It could work. At least that's what Dean believed before the bombs actually dropped and his suit led him to murder a Very Important Man at the foot of a blackened obelisk. Now D.C. is looking awfully empty. Life on Earth is pretty much coming to an end. All of which leaves Dean with a single question-"What now?" The answer to that question will take him on an uncanny voyage across a newly nuclear America where he must confront the problems associated with loneliness, radiation, love, and an ever-evolving cockroach suit with a mind of its own. Dean's bizarre adventures mark the last chronicle of human existence, the final entries in our species' own...

"Night of the Assholes" Kevin L. Donihe - From Wonderland Award Winner Kevin L. Donihe, comes a hilarious tribute to Night of the Living Dead A plague of assholes is infecting the countryside. Normal everyday people are transforming into jerks, snobs, dicks, and douchebags. And they all have only one purpose: to make your life a living hell. The assholes are everywhere. They're picking fights, causing accidents, and even killing people. But she must remain calm. If you raise your temper to an asshole you'll become one of them. After losing her brother to the asshole onslaught, Barbara flees for her life. She finds safety in a desolate farmhouse with six other survivors. Cut off from the world and surrounded by a sea of assholes, they must figure out a way to last through the night. But more and more of those annoying bastards are gathering outside, preparing for the coming of something much worse. . .

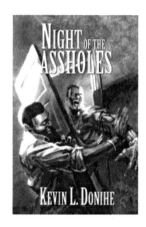

"Bullet Through Your Face" Edward Lee - No writer is more extreme, perverted, or gross than Edward Lee. His world is one of psychopathic redneck rapists, sex addicted demons, and semen stealing aliens. Brace yourself, the king of splatterspunk is guaranteed to shock, offend, and make you laugh until you vomit. *Bullet Through Your Face* collects three novellas demonstrating Lee's mind-blasting talent. "Ever Nat" - One man is forced to endure an unimaginable torment just to stay alive, one night at a time. "The Salt-Diviner" - A touching story of one couple and the quadriplegic, homeless fortune teller locked in their basement. "The Refrigerator Full of Sperm" - Why are all the men of Luntville falling into comas with their pants down and dicks up?

"Apeshit" Carlton Mellick III - *Apeshit* is Mellick's love letter to the great and terrible B-horror movie genre. Six trendy teenagers (three cheerleaders and three football players) go to an isolated cabin in the mountains for a weekend of drinking, partying, and crazy sex, only to find themselves in the middle of a life and death struggle against a horribly mutated psychotic freak that just won't stay dead. Mellick parodies this horror cliché and twists it into something deeper and stranger. It is the literary equivalent of a grindhouse film. It is a splatterpunk's wet dream. It is perhaps one of the most fucked up books ever written. If you are a fan of Takashi Miike, Evil Dead, or Eurotrash horror then you must read this book.

"Extinction Journals" Jeremy Robert Johnson - You can survive a nuclear blast. All you need is some luck, and maybe a customized business suit coated in cockroaches. It could work. At least that's what Dean believed before the bombs actually dropped and his suit led him to murder a Very Important Man at the foot of a blackened obelisk. Now D.C. is looking awfully empty. Life on Earth is pretty much coming to an end. All of which leaves Dean with a single question-"What now?" The answer to that question will take him on an uncanny voyage across a newly nuclear America where he must confront the problems associated with loneliness, radiation, love, and an ever-evolving cockroach suit with a mind of its own. Dean's bizarre adventures mark the last chronicle of human existence, the final entries in our species' own… Extinction Journals

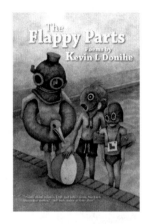

"The Flappy Parts" Kevin L. Donihe - Collecting the best poems written over the last decade by Wonderland Award-winning author Kevin L. Donihe, *The Flappy Parts* is a gonzo journey through the nightmare absurdities of modern life. But even as undead midgets rise from the grave and nymphomaniac computers rape human beings, Kevin L. Donihe points us toward a stranger and better future. He shows us that between Heaven and Hell, it's all about The Flappy Parts.

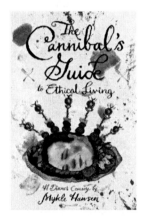

"The Cannibal's Guide to Ethical Living" Mykle Hansen - In a remote and dangerous corner of the ocean, the renowned gourmet and food journalist Louis De Gustibus is held captive by an elite chef—and vegan cannibal—named André. But André would never eat his dear friend Louis. Andre only eats millionaires! Over a five star French meal of fine wine, organic vegetables and human flesh, a lunatic delivers a witty, chilling, disturbingly sane argument in favor of eating the rich. It's a darkly hilarious dessert to Pollan's The Omnivore's Dilemma and Foer's Eating Animals—a tale of good and evil, of rich and poor, of manners, madness and meat.

"The Baby Jesus Butt Plug" Carlton Mellick III - WARNING: DO NOT MOLEST THE BABY JESUS! Step into a dark and absurd world where human beings are slaves to corporations, people are photocopied instead of born, and the baby jesus is a very popular anal probe. Presented in the style of a children's fairy tale, *The Baby Jesus Butt Plug* is a short dystopian horror story about a young couple who make the mistake of buying a living clone of the baby jesus to use for anal sex. Once the baby jesus clone turns on them, all hell breaks loose.

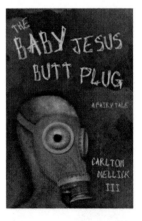

"Brain Cheese Buffet" Edward Lee - You've seen Cannibal Holocaust. You've seen Salo. You've seen Nekromantik. You ain't seen shit! Zombie prostitutes, religious rapists, horny werewolves, death by vomit, and sexual fetishes scraped off the sidewalk. From sex prisons to mafia torture chambers, hold on tight because you're about to enter the perverted and twisted mind of Edward Lee. Once you've seen what he has to show you - there's no coming back. *Brain Cheese Buffet* collects nine of Lee's most sought after tales of violence and body fluids. Featuring the Stoker nominated "Mr. Torso," the legendary gross-out piece "the Dritiphilist," the notorious "The McCrath Model SS40-C, Series S," and six more stories to test your gag reflex.

"The Book of a Thousand Sins" Wrath James White - God's a mean bastard and doesn't give a shit about you. Welcome to a world of Zombie nymphomaniacs, psychopathic deities, voodoo surgery, and murderous priests. A place where the gate to Heaven is in an elderly whore's pussy and shit covered sewer drains lead to Hell. Where mutilation sex clubs are in vogue and torture machines are sex toys. This is the mind of Wrath James White. No one makes it out alive - not even God himself. *The Book of a Thousand Sins* collects fifteen anti-faith tales of depravity, gore, and sex from the celebrated master of hardcore horror. Be warned; Wrath James White is here to scar you.

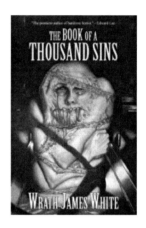

"Zombies and Shit" Carlton Mellick III - Battle Royale meets Return of the Living Dead in this post-apocalyptic action adventure Twenty people wake to find themselves in a boarded-up building in the middle of the zombie wasteland. They soon realize they have been chosen as contestants on a popular reality show called Zombie Survival. Each contestant is given a backpack of supplies and a unique weapon. Their goal: be the first to make it through the zombie-plagued city to the pick-up zone alive. But because there's only one seat available on the helicopter, the contestants not only have to fight off the hordes of the living dead, they must also fight each other. *Zombies and Shit* is Mellick's craziest book to date. A campy, trashy, punk rock gore fest that is as funny as it is brutal, as sad as it is strange. An edge-of-your-seat thrill ride that twists the zombie genre into something you've never seen before.

"Piecemeal June" Jordan Krall - Kevin lives in a small apartment above a porn shop with his tarot-reading cat, Mithra. He has gotten used to Mithra bringing him things from outside: dead mice, Twinkie wrappers, donut scraps, houseplants, and the occasional rabbit head. But one day, Mithra brings him an ankle... a sweaty piece of rubber-latex shaped like a human ankle. Later, he is brought an eyeball, then a foot. After more latex body parts are brought upstairs, Kevin decides to glue them together to form a piecemeal sex doll. But once the last piece is glued into place, the sex doll comes to life. She says her name is June. She comes from another world and is on the run from an evil pornographer and three crab-human hybrid assassins. *Piecemeal June* is a reality-bending journey into love, sex, death, and a bizarre parallel world of butchered flesh.

"The Cannibals of Candyland" Carlton Mellick III - There exists a race of cannibals who are made out of candy. They live in an underground world filled with lollipop forests and gumdrop goblins. During the day, while you are away at work, they come above ground and prowl our streets for food. Their prey: your children. They lure young boys and girls to them with their sweet scent and bright colorful candy coating, then rip them apart with razor sharp teeth and claws. When he was a child, Franklin Pierce witnessed the death of his siblings at the hands of a candy woman with pink cotton candy hair. Since that day, the candy people have become his obsession. He has spent his entire life trying to prove that they exist. And after discovering the entrance to the underground world of the candy people, Franklin finds himself venturing into their sugary domain. His mission: capture one of them and bring it back, dead or alive.

"Starfish Girl" Athena Villaverde - In a post-apocalyptic underwater dome, there lives a girl with a starfish growing from her head. Her name is Ohime. She is the starfish girl. Alone in this world, Ohime must fight for her life against lecherous crabmen, piranha people, and a yellow algae that is causing humans to mutate into fish. Until she meets Timbre, a woman with deadly sea anemone hair. Ohime thinks she is safe with her new protector and friend, but Timbre is on the run from a violent past. Now they must escape Timbre's former master, the evil Dr. Ichii, who is determined to conquer the underwater dome . . . and destroy the starfish girl and her friend in the process.

"Mr. Magic Realism" Bruce Taylor - Welcome to the wonderful world of Mr. Magic Realism. AMAZING FEATS! A man hangs from the rafters of his house by only his thumbs for over a decade. BEWILDERING MYSTERIES! A mall that might be the afterlife is stormed by giant insects. COMICAL FANTASIES! Aliens on the run hide out in American breakfast foods. DAZZLING NIGHTMARES! Spiders put a man on trial for crimes he has not committed. Like Golden Age science fiction comics written by Freud, Mr. Magic Realism is a strange, insightful adventure that spans the furthest reaches of the galaxy, exploring the hidden caverns in the hearts and minds of men, women, aliens, and biomechanical cats.

"Sorry I Ruined Your Orgy" Bradley Sands - Bizarro humorist Bradley Sands returns with one of the strangest, most hilarious collections of the year. In *Sorry I Ruined Your Orgy*, the pope gets sued, a headless man falls in love with a bowl of rice, and architects dismantle the earth. A war breaks out over greeting cards. A suicidal amputee tries to kill himself. William S. Burroughs becomes an amateur archaeologist and Tao Lin drinks an ape-flavored smoothie. Between a breakfast of clocks, a lunch date with Adolf Hitler, and breakdancing in outer space, anything is possible in the work of Bradley Sands. Just never wear a bear costume to an orgy.

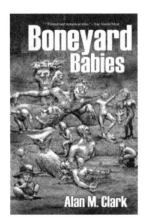

"Boneyard Babies" Alan M. Clark - *Boneyard babies, gather round! Come suckle the Musty Cow's Teat of Death!* A man searches for his lover in a medical laboratory where people are transformed into nightmarish mutants. An undead prostitute enters the underworld to face off against a jackal-headed god. A woman incarcerated for her lipstick addiction must eat her own limbs or face imminent death. A tumor recounts its life with a man named Applewide. In the morbidly surreal universe of World Fantasy Award-winner Alan M. Clark, there are only two types of people: those who are monsters, and those who are eaten by monsters. Proceed with caution.

"Rampaging Fuckers of Everything on the Crazy Shitting Planet of the Vomit Atmosphere" Mykle Hansen - With the wit of Christopher Moore, the inventiveness of Terry Gilliam and the rudeness of South Park, comes the Rampaging Fuckers of Everything on the Crazy Shitting Planet of the Vomit Atmosphere, an award-winning collection of three short novels by a master of satire. Hansen's surreal fiction is ridiculously fun to read. His subversive tales capture the smugness of mainstream culture, as he thrusts his characters into absurd and humorous situations that reveal the defects in the modern social fabric. A must read for fans of weird humor.

"Jack and Mr. Grin" Andersen Prunty - A surreal and horrifying thriller from Andersen Prunty. Jack Orange is a twenty-something guy who works at a place called The Tent packing dirt in boxes and shipping them off to exotic, unheard of locales. He thinks about his girlfriend, Gina Black, and the ring he hopes to surprise her with. But when he returns home one day, Gina isn't there. He receives a strange call from a man who sounds like he is smiling- Mr. Grin. He says he has Gina. He gives Jack twenty-four hours to find her. What follows is Jack's bizarre journey through an increasingly warped and surreal landscape where an otherworldly force burns brands into those he comes in contact with, trains appear out of thin air, rooms turn themselves inside out and computers are powered by birds. And if he does find Gina, how will he ever survive a grueling battle to the death with Mr. Grin?

"Ocean of Lard" Carlton Mellick III and Kevin L. Donihe - You're on the run from the cops and need to disappear somehow. Luckily you happen across a secret ocean in the middle of Wyoming. An undiscovered world of pirates and zombies that, according to maps, couldn't possibly exist. But here it is, a vast white sea that is made of some kind of greasy blubber substance instead of water. To escape, you must join the crew of one of the two ships at the dock. The first is a strange black cube-shaped vessel called The Eye World and the other is a totally punk rock pirate ship called The Rotten Sore. Which will you take? If you board The Eye World, turn to page 21. If you take The Rotten Sore, turn to page 22. But choose wisely! You could find yourself screwing demonic faeries and a cyborg dominatrix on top of a pile of treasure, or you could end up as lunch for a team of floating telepathic walrus heads.

CPSIA information can be obtained at www.ICGtesting.com

263728BV00002B/96/P